THE
REVENGE
OF THE
OKORIES

THE REVENGE OF THE OKORIES

CHARLES GP KRAMER

Published under licence by Brown Dog Books and
The Self-Publishing Partnership, 7 Green Park Station, Bath BA1 1JB

www.selfpublishingpartnership.co.uk

ISBN printed book: 978-1-83952-189-8
ISBN e-book: 978-1-83952-190-4

Cover design by Daniel Styler
Internal design by Andrew Easton

Printed and bound in the UK
This book is printed on FSC certified paper

Dawn and the Knight: A reluctant soldier
What Did Eye See
Errs and Places: An Autobiography

Acknowledgements and Dedication

It would be very remiss of me not to mention my dear 'lil sis' Jane Brook. It was she who took my first book in this set of three and worked hard for me, not just correcting my mistakes but showing where I could make the story a little more interesting.

It seems strange calling someone I actually haven't met in person a good friend but she is a fellow author and wrote a superb book called *The Overcoming*. Chris Elmes has read all of my work, casting a critical eye and giving sound advice that I value.

My thanks go to my dear adopted grandson Daniel Ogilvie who has done most of the illustrations. Also, my thanks go to Daniel Williams Art for producing the artwork for my first book.

Dedicated to my dearest wife Sue, my family and to my dear, sweet Jane Fletcher: sister-in-law, friend and the one who found my humour funny, sadly taken from us far too early aged 49 and two days.

Foreword

Many years ago, I wrote an autobiography to let my three children know why I was frequently telling them off. In reality, a parent is only a page ahead in the book of life, and I wanted them to know where I went wrong as a youngster. I hoped that they wouldn't endanger themselves and make the same mistakes. As it turned out, it was an exercise in futility. The book had been enjoyed by many, resulting in my being encouraged to write my first novel, *Dawn and the Knight*.

The novel began as a trilogy about the main characters in book one, but having written several thousands of words in each of the books, my son accidentally trashed the computer, and I lost the lot apart from about six thousand words that I had printed off on an old dot matrix printer. Having enjoyed writing that first novel, I decided to write the second (*What Did Eye See?*), and because it left me feeling that it left too many loose ends, I felt the need to write a third and final novel.

All three are related in some way and I hope the reader derives some pleasure from reading them.

The Revenge of the Okories

PROLOGUE

It was in the early 70s when a little-known West African billionaire called Afolabi Okorie set his sights on the United Kingdom. He wanted a base in a quiet corner of the country for his arms-smuggling business and other illicit activities. To begin with, he had hired small groups of three operatives, and one of these groups was headed up by a person called Heinrich Moeller. He was in fact called Bernhardt von Austerlitz and a West German intelligence officer who had infiltrated the gang after disposing of the previous group leader. He managed to convince the organisation that he was capable of taking over.

It had been leaked that Cranfield University, together with German scientists, had developed some highly sophisticated sniper sights. They were capable of penetrating exceptionally thick undergrowth with very little risk of being detected and Okorie wanted them. Once von Austerlitz (*aka* Heinrich Moeller) had secured them, the three of them hid away in a quiet corner of England in a town called Gosport.

It had been prearranged that Okorie's luxury yacht called the *Ardent Voyager* would be moored off the Isle of Wight between certain dates, where the three would send a signal for a small launch to come ashore at Stokes Bay to collect them.

Just after settling in, one of the gang called Jürgen had been befriended by a person called James Adams who von Austerlitz suspected was a CIA agent. Fearful that Adams could jeopardise the operation, he had orchestrated an argument in his home and killed him.

To complicate matters further, the murder was witnessed by a young boy called Stuart who, along with his friend George, was avenging the loss of their football that von Austerlitz had speared with a garden fork. Stuart was about to post a pack of dog muck retrieved from the bins through his door. He had heard the argument and the scream, and in panic he let the flap snap sharply on his fingers causing him to scream in shock. This alerted the inhabitants. Being too curious for their own good, George, who lived opposite von Austerlitz, asked his young sister to watch the house for when they would leave and return. Their chance came one afternoon, and they entered the house by the back door. The gang returned and trapped them both in the house where the boys were taken and ended up on-board the *Ardent Voyager* bound for Africa.

Extract from the evening edition of the *British News Journal*.
Amos McKenzie reports:

There was frenzied activity on the River Thames last evening because what at first appeared to be a log floating along the South Bank was in fact a body.

This was followed a short while later by a further two bodies, both of which had their hands bound behind their backs and shot through the head. A spokesman for the Met, in a statement to the press, said it seemed most likely that it was a gangland execution and that the perpetrators would be hunted down and brought to justice.

The Police Commissionaire has called for calm and the Chief Constable will be giving a press conference in the morning.

The identities of the bodies who are all male (two white and one black); are not yet known and there have been no reports of any missing persons.

The bodies were taken to the public mortuary in Croydon where post-mortems will be carried out.

Urgent message despatched from Major Charles Bradley to WO David Murphy within one hour of the bodies being recovered, and before the story was released to the press:

FAO WO2 D MURPHY:

Sergeant Major Murphy, it is with regret I must inform you that owing to a situation that has arisen, you will need to reschedule your leave. I have tried to call you personally but have been unable to make contact.

My sincere apologies since I know you have earned a break, but you are required to report for duty immediately.

Major C Bradley.

Chapter 1

David Murphy was suddenly awoken with a start; he had recovered almost immediately from his slumbers as he became aware that someone was in his house. Carefully, he cast his bedsheets aside, quietly extricated himself from the bed and crept towards the door. There he waited.

His senses were in overdrive, his hearing had become acute and, although his heart was beating frantically, he managed to stay calm which the training in Special Forces had taught him.

There was no mistaking a barely audible creak on the penultimate step leading to the landing.

Murky, as he was known, had already taken hold of his favoured weapon, a Fairbairn Sykes which is a lethal dagger. He stood away from the door and waited just to the side of the entrance.

As if from nowhere, he felt the coldness of a blade that was touching the soft tissue of his throat; he was unable to prevent the knife from sliding across and he saw his lifeblood pouring onto the floor.

He looked down and saw the blood wasn't actually his, but that of a mutilated body that was bleeding from every square inch of skin and was writhing in agony.

Murky was now properly awake, sweating profusely with his breath rasping and heart beating wildly.

It had been a recurring nightmare that had begun several

months before. Two years had passed since he and five other men had stormed a warehouse which was the headquarters of the Urban Commando Group. They were about to unleash a horde of armed men onto the streets of London causing death and havoc. Originally, it was a decoy to hide the real crime of stealing four of the most expensive diamonds on loan from four private exhibitors.

He knew the cause of this nightmare: one of the group, a very popular man and personal friend called Ben, had been reconnoitring the warehouse prior to the attack but was caught and tortured horribly by a West African called Afolabi Okorie. Ben had been sadistically cut to ribbons, dismembered and left to bleed to death. It was Murky who had found him just before he died as he held him in his arms. Murky and another friend, George O'Rourke, had travelled to Ghana and had exacted their revenge on him.

Things seemed to have settled down for a while and he had enjoyed a secondment to the USA where he worked closely with the DEA and it wasn't until his return that the nightmares began.

On returning home after his deployment, he decided to take a well-earned rest and was planning to meet his Polish girlfriend Ingrid at Stansted Airport. She was flying in from Lublin in Poland where she worked as a production manager in a chemical and pharmaceutical company and was due to land at two-thirty that day. They intended to spend two glorious weeks together in the Lake District. It was Murky's turn to host the break because the previous holiday they'd had together was in the Bieszczady Mountains in Poland.

They had been dating each other on and off over the last five years but in the last twelve months, Ingrid had started to get serious and made it plain that she wanted to settle down with Murky and have a family.

Murky for his part was thinking that it was time to leave the Armed Forces, having served twenty-two years of distinguished service.

Having been partly instrumental in helping to prevent the attack in London, he had been promoted from Staff Sergeant to Warrant

Officer second class. With the extra money of the promotion, the money saved whilst in America and together with the cash he had put to one side over the years, he found himself in the envious position of being reasonably well off.

He had invested in three properties which he let out, giving him a considerable income with only one mortgage outstanding that he could pay off with a portion of his gratuity.

At the age of 40, he realised he wasn't as quick as he used to be and needed his sleep more and knew it definitely *was* time to leave.

His friend Jonah who had served with him had a thriving grocery business in Fareham and offered Murky a job, but he gratefully declined the offer, saying it was a little too tame for him.

Jonah had been wounded in the kneecap during the raid on the Urban Commandos which at the time looked as though he would need crutches. As it turned out, the surgeons did a superb job on repairing the knee, leaving him with just a slight limp.

Once he had composed himself, he went to have a shower and get some breakfast before driving to Stansted Airport. Every time he had this nightmare, he found it difficult to shake it from his mind and would watch children's television just to see something pleasant as he ate breakfast; his favourite was Shaun the Sheep. Today, however, he didn't have the time as he had to leave and take his old van around to his parents' house to collect his Citroën C5. He knew they would want him to stay for a bite to eat and a chat since he hadn't been to see them for several weeks.

They lived about an hour away in Andover where they had recently moved to from Alton. As it was on his way, he felt obliged to at least stay for coffee and a snack.

Once he had collected his car and suffered his mother's fussing, he left for the airport and, although he was looking forward to having a break away with Ingrid, he was still feeling the affect of his nightmare.

It normally always filled him with paranoia for the whole day but on this occasion, there was something else. He wasn't able to put his finger on it, but there was something that had triggered a sixth sense in his inner self. It was something he seemed to have developed over the years and he knew there was something very, very wrong with this day.

Try as he may, he wasn't able to shake it off as he drove along the M3. He had convinced himself that he was being followed, and as much as he tried to pass it off as an unjustified suspicion, there was definitely a car that had been behind him for some considerable time. In fact, he first casually noticed it on joining the A34 as he drove to his parents' house. He tried to tell himself that it can't have been the same one because he had spent a good hour and a half with his mum and dad making it most unlikely to be the same one. However, no matter how much he reasoned with himself, it was a green Volkswagen Golf and there weren't many that he had seen of that colour.

Still feeling uneasy, he decided to indicate and pull onto the hard shoulder and see whether or not it would prompt the car behind to do the same. To his relief, the car drove past without apparently paying any attention to Murky. He waited there a short while and then indicated, accelerated to the general speed of the traffic and rejoined the M3.

Still feeling vulnerable, he tried to take his mind off his feeling of malaise, planning in his head how he would be spending the next two weeks with Ingrid. He had bought a beautiful diamond ring since he decided that he would propose to her over a romantic dinner in their room that evening.

He had booked them both into The Swan Hotel and Spa Windermere, having explained to the concierge what he intended to do, and who, in return, promised him a very special room.

Murky wasn't the easiest person to make contact with when on leave since he never used a landline. He only possessed a mobile phone which he always turned off at the start of his holiday and therefore had no idea he was required to report for duty.

He pulled into Fleet Services for a comfort break, having been plied with several cups of tea.

On looking around, he noticed there was a green Volkswagen

Golf setting his senses into overdrive; however, as he left his car to enter the services area, there was one other of identical colour which put his mind at rest slightly. He still had a nagging feeling in the back of his head and wasn't able to shake it off.

Once he had relieved himself, he made his way back to the car and decided, as a precaution, to move it to a more obscure position and wait to see which of the green Volkswagens moved out first.

He didn't have to wait long: two people left shortly after and began to look around in earnest, then got into one of the cars and sped off back onto the M3.

Murky now knew there was something amiss and sat thinking about his next move. He didn't have the luxury of time since Ingrid's plane was due to arrive in two and a half hours and, although he still had plenty of time to get to Stansted Airport, he had to make allowances for traffic etc., not to mention what lay ahead with the two men who had been following him.

He decided that he would catch up with the cars but keep a safe distance behind and just keep an eye out for any moves they may decide to take.

After a couple of miles at 85 miles an hour, he realised that the occupants of the car must have panicked, because they were nowhere in sight and so he accelerated to one hundred. He hoped he wouldn't be pulled over because his explanation would be seen to be lame to say the least.

Finally, he saw them in the distance and so he kept a safe distance behind and watched.

They did seem to be in a hurry but Murky kept the course and saw that they both eventually left the M3 at Junction 3 and so Murky slowed and pulled onto the hard shoulder putting his hazard lights on briefly and waited.

He assumed that if the car *was* following him, and judging by the way they were driving, they must have panicked, thinking they had missed him and so decided to double-back.

Once he was satisfied that they were long gone, he pulled out and made his way to the airport. The rest of his journey was uneventful.

He parked and made his way to the Arrivals lounge, venturing into the Burger King for some lunch.

He wracked his brains trying to work out who his 'would-be' assailants were if they were indeed intent on harming him. He also wondered that if he had been under surveillance, how long had it been going on?

He was deep in thought when he heard the explosion and the unmistakeable sound of small arms fire followed by screams of panicking people.

Thinking quickly, he ran to the tall menu board and stood behind it taking a peek in the direction of the noise where he saw one of the armed police officers lying very still on the floor. There was no sign of his companion but calmly walking in his direction was the perpetrator, casually changing the magazine on his gun.

He then darted back to the counter and told the member of staff who seemed transfixed to the spot to pour him some boiling hot water in a mug and to hand him a sharp knife.

'NOW!' he shouted, bringing the staff member out of his trance. He obediently did as he was told and then Murky told him to get the rest of the staff as far back into the cooking area as he could and lie as flat as they were able on the floor.

Using the sharp knife, he made a small incision in the menu board and waited as the gunman approached who was just shooting indiscriminately at anything that moved.

He was getting very near to Murky's position and someone in the eating area who was hiding with a child under a table screamed. This attracted the gunman to get even nearer and just as he cleared the menu board, Murky sprang into action.

He jumped out in front of him which took the gunman completely by surprise and threw the boiling water straight into his face. He howled in agony but still had a hold of the weapon, so Murky felt he had no choice but to quickly stand to one side of the gunman, thrusting the knife deep into his midriff under the protective vest.

The man fell like a stone, releasing the gun and trying to reach for a grenade but Murky was on him in a flash, preventing any further carnage.

Within minutes, the area was teeming with armed officers and Murky being ordered to lie flat on the ground with his arms spread so his hands could be seen.

Once he was hauled to his feet and his identity established, he told the police that there was possibly another assailant somewhere explaining his concern about the Volkswagen Golf. An extensive search of the car park, however, revealed that there weren't any remotely meeting that description.

It did seem strange to Murky that the car almost met the same description as the one that had tried to kill his friend George O'Rourke some years earlier. It was all linked to something he had unknowingly witnessed in Ann's Hill Cemetery and to a known criminal called Afolabi Okorie. But even more confusing was the fact that the gang he had been funding was completely destroyed by Murky, George and a few others, ending with Okorie being killed by the two of them. It was an act of such heroism; it had earned Murky and Ben a Military Medal (Ben's being awarded posthumously. He had been brutally murdered by Afolabi Okorie and Murky and George followed him to Ghana where they killed him along with three of his henchmen). Jonah and George for their part, being civilians, albeit still on the Reserve List, received the George Cross.

Murky was also offered a commission and not for the first time turned it down. A great deal of pressure was put on him, but he always gave the same reason: being a staff officer would entail more time in an office than being in the thick of all the action.

Because of the act of violence, Ingrid's plane along with all other arrivals had been diverted to London Central Airport.

Murky was clearly shaken and in a state of total confusion. Was the Volkswagen linked to this in some way? If so, why wasn't it in the car park?

He had managed to get a glimpse of the two men at Fleet Services and didn't think that the gunman remotely resembled either of them.

Once he had cleared his head, he turned on his mobile phone and decided to ring Major Bradley and noticed that there had been several missed calls from him.

'Hello, sir, it's WO Murphy and I have just noticed you have been trying to contact me. My apologies but as you know, I rarely have my mobile on when I'm on leave.'

'Murky, we have a big problem and you are required to report for duty immediately. I am not prepared to discuss it over the phone, but can you come in as soon as possible?'

'I will be there as soon as I can, but Ingrid's plane has been diverted to London City and I need to let her know what is happening.'

'I have already despatched a driver to the airport to collect her for you and we will put her up in a hotel and you can chat to her after the briefing, but can you get here with all haste?'

Once he had finished with the security staff and police, he made his way back to his car and drove straight to the meeting.

Chapter 2

On arrival, he was immediately ushered into the major's office and was surprised to see Emma Belchin in the room together with Brendan Taylor from MI6 whom he had worked with before on the Urban Commando case. Also, in the room were two other men who were introduced as Jeremy Fisher and Steve Docherty whom Murky also knew from Special Forces. Both belonged to the SBS.

Charles addressed the group, saying that they all knew one another and decided to get straight down to business.

'Right, people, apologies for dragging you all in at such short notice and at the moment today is only a briefing but there may be a need to mobilise you within an hour to tackle what is at present a perceived threat to this country.'

He then beckoned to Emma Belchin who had a picture of a magnificent luxury ocean-going yacht up on the screen.

'I imagine some of you may recognise the lines of this launch.'

Murky immediately blurted out that it looked like the *Ardent Voyager*!'

'I thought she had been impounded and was going to be sold off at auction next year!'

'That's very true, Murky, but this isn't the *Voyager*, it's her sister ship called the *Ardent Ventura* and belongs to a gentleman called Adwin Okorie. Does that name ring any bells?'

There was silence in the room and so Emma continued.

'He is the older brother of Afolabi Okorie. They were both the youngest of five children and it seems that because the parents favoured Afolabi, the three older siblings picked on him and it was Adwin who did his best to protect him from the others. But when the two youngsters grew up, their older brothers had all been mysteriously killed. It is widely believed that they were bumped off by Afolabi and Adwin, and if you think Afolabi was evil, you cannot begin to imagine how vicious and totally sadistic Adwin is reported to be.

Murky needed more information and said, 'I have some questions. Firstly, do we think he is up to more mischief and does he operate in the same way as his brother? If he does, can we expect to see some subterfuge which he would employ in hiding his real intentions?'

'We do know a great deal about him, but unfortunately, we have no clue as to where the Ventura is headed or what Adwin might be up to. This picture was taken about four miles out from the mouth of the Pra River by a Ghanaian military aircraft. Ever since the furore caused between Britain and the Ghanaian authorities over Afolabi's shenanigans, the family have been kept under surveillance by their government. It seems that the situation with Afolabi highlighted quite a bit of corruption within the family, but without any tangible evidence against them, Adwin is free do as he pleases. Like his brother, he is an immensely wealthy man. He is as involved as his brother in all that he dealt with, but it is rumoured he funds terror groups around Africa, targeting democratically elected governments by putting in a group of terrorists to try and destabilise the country. It seems that when things look bad for those specific countries, he then funds a group of mercenaries to do away with the terrorists whom he originally recruited, and since "by doing away with them" is in fact a euphemism for using the same group of terrorists but standing under a different banner, they claim to be the mercenaries to bring back stability. I might add, it seems it leaves grateful ministers paying him large sums of money to basically to allow them to remain in power. Just how grateful these governments actually are is debatable since it's believed that he threatens them with the removal of his mercenaries. It is in fact one of the biggest protection rackets I have ever come across.'

Just then, there was a knock at the door when Major Bradley's clerk, a corporal, handed him a note. He excused himself from those present and briefly read through and he looked up at Murky.

'It would seem that the incident you dealt with at Stansted Airport has nothing at all to do with the green Volkswagens that you felt were following you. The person in question was called Jacob Reynolds who lived fairly locally to Stansted in a town called Saffron Walden. By all accounts he was a loner who had a fascination for weapons. The police raided his flat and found a great deal of incriminating evidence, but it is most unlikely that he was linked to a terrorist group.'

'You refer to him in the past tense, so I assume that he died?'

'He did, Murky, he was still alive when he was secured, but despite trying to keep him alive, he bled out on the way to hospital. The stab wound you administered went very deep and hit some vitals.'

Murky thought for a while when Major Bradley again spoke.

'We are, however, very concerned about the green VWs since it appears it is a vehicle of choice by a group we thought to be completely disbanded. It would appear that the Urban Commandos are becoming a nuisance again. If you remember, it was the type of vehicle that nearly killed George O'Rourke some years ago and this does rather link into why you have all been called here at such short notice today.'

'Last night, three bodies were all retrieved from the River Thames and they had all been executed. Two of the victims were from MI6 and the other, a certain Kwabena Darkenoo from the Ghanaian military, had infiltrated the group a week ago and contact was lost almost immediately. We have been advised that a resurgent Urban Commando Group have been contacted by Okorie and all we have been able to glean is what we believe to be some kind of code word. It is nonsensical at the moment, but a conversation was overheard with the word "RHYMOW". Adwin has been kept under a watchful eye but about four months ago, he started to specialise in deep sea diving and has been recruiting specialists in that area. It was for this reason that the two chaps from MI6 had volunteered for the mission to try and find out what, if anything, is being planned. Derek Walters and Edward Finnegan were both ex-SBS and experts in deep sea diving, but what alerted Adwin to their identities we have no idea. If you recall, all previous attempts at infiltrating the Urban Commandos never really got past the first twenty-four hours, leading us to suspect that there might be a leak within the agencies with whom we are cooperating. It is being looked into as we speak but we still have absolutely no idea what is being planned but we suspect that London will once again be a target.'

'Just an aside, sir, but on thinking about it, the VW that I thought was following me was an 'R' registration. If I remember correctly that was the same registration as the one that attacked George which was never traced.'

The room acknowledged the comment which led them to confirm that the Urban Commandos were indeed becoming more involved than was initially suspected and that Okorie was at the bottom of it all.

Charles Bradley then asked for ideas of possible targets that would involve diving specialists in an attack against the heart of London.

'I imagine it will involve somewhere in the Thames but that's a really long river to police!'

Murky was curious and he asked to be reminded what was thought to be the code word Adwin was using.

'"RHYMOW" but we are uncertain whether or not this is the correct spelling since it has only been received by word of mouth.'

Charles Bradley then said that since it was all they had to go on at the moment, there was precious little that they could do.

'What happens next depends on what the group decide to do so in the meantime, and once again my apologies for dragging you all here for the briefing but you all need to be ready to move at very short notice.'

The meeting was dismissed but Murky was requested to remain once all the others had left the room.

'Sorry about this, Murky, I know you have earned this leave but this potential threat to the UK, the suspicious VW together with your expertise, I'm afraid we will have to have you easily reachable just in case we need you fairly rapidly. George has taken some leave and he and Jayne are visiting his sister in America. I feel they are safe enough there because it seems that Okorie has a grudge against Great Britain. The best we can offer, I'm afraid, is that you collect Inky from where we have put her and you'll both be driven to the local airport where we will deliver you both by helicopter to the… Er, where was it now? Ah! The Swan Hotel and Spa Windermere, wasn't it?'

Murky was about to protest but the major held up his hand to stop him from saying anything.

'I know you are aware of our procedures, Murky, but I'm afraid that this is an order. There will be operatives in the vicinity to ensure not only your safety, but Ingrid's as well. The thing is, we know you are more than capable of looking after yourself but you would not be able to keep your eyes on Ingrid twenty-four-seven; if anyone was able to get to her while your back was turned, it would most definitely compromise your ability to react. Don't worry, my boy, they will be inconspicuous, and I promise you will not even know they are there. The team is to comprise two males and two females who will be staying at the hotel.'

'With respect, sir, I wasn't going to protest about having agents nearby but I am concerned about George's safety because it may not just be a grudge against the UK but also a personal one against George and me. I am convinced that with a little bit of digging within Okorie's organisation, it would show that we were in the vicinity at the time of his brother's death. I would bet ten to one that Adwin knew his brother better than to go out for a drive with his cronies to a remote part of the country, get drunk and accidentally burn themselves to a pile of ashes, especially in a car that he didn't even own! Not only that, the car was hired by George and you can rest assured that Adwin knows beyond any shadow of doubt who, I won't say 'murdered', but executed his younger brother. I am left in no doubt that he is not only coming for us, but to punish London as well: the family lost a lot of credibility over the incident a couple of years ago. We both know that the authorities felt it expedient to report the incident as a result of a drunken orgy because he had become an embarrassment to them. There is, of course the added problem that George was on the Late Show with David Letterman last night with Stuart and Katie, so if there is going to be another attempt on his life, Okorie now knows where he is.'

The major acknowledged Murky's concern and said he would get on to his American counterpart to see if at this late stage something could be done.

Chapter 3

Stuart and Katie were enjoying a renaissance in America and their appearance was the talk of the town. They were in great demand since they had both developed a double act which was first aired on the Late Show with David Letterman a few years earlier and they became an instant hit with the American public. Their zany humour and banter turned them into a formidable team, and so after Katie had given birth to Georgie (named after her brother George), they had gone back to the States to commence their second tour.

George and Jayne had just started their holiday with Stuart and Katie when a request was made for them to all to go on the Late Show with David Letterman.

It seemed a strange request but obviously the researchers had been busy learning about them being kidnapped together by an arms-smuggling gang and whisked off to Africa. Their appearance was scheduled for two nights later.

It seemed that Stuart and Katie were very calm but both the O'Rourkes were quite nervous about appearing publicly. They were consoled by Stuart's admission that it was the same for them and assured them both that once the programme had started, they would soon settle down because Dave Letterman was very good at making the atmosphere tranquil and serene. It did help but the nerves didn't really subside until just before the show: George made it clear that no reference should be made regarding his work with Special Forces or with any of the operations he had been involved with, but was happy to talk about their time with Bernhard von Austerlitz and subsequent rescue by Danny Knight and Hendrik Van Hove. Dave Letterman already had two other guests, but because of the popularity of Stuart and Katie, he wanted them on last to end his show on a high note. Finally, they were called forward to where they waited for Dave Letterman to introduce them and paused anxiously for the announcement.

'Ladies and gentlemen, it gives me the greatest pleasure to bring on my last guests for this evening: please welcome back to America Stuart and Katie Baxter and Katie's brother George O'Rourke and his wife Jayne.'

There was rapturous applause since this was the Baxters' first appearance in three years and the Americans had never forgotten how entertaining and funny they were.

Once sat down, Dave Letterman firstly said how pleased everybody was to have the Baxters back but then asked the question about how they got involved with a terrorist group.

'So, let's get this straight, you were both kidnapped and then whisked off to Africa. I mean who on earth manages to do something like that?

Katie chipped in, saying that they only had two brain cells between them: one for breathing in and one for breathing out.

'That's rich!' George retorted. 'That must mean you don't have one at all because you were involved just as much as we were!'

George was chuckling at his remark and mentioned that she was the worst 'lookout' in history.

Stuart just looked at him because, being forever serious, he rarely ever got involved in banter while Katie sat there with her mouth wide open.

'You seem to forget, dear brother, that I was very young and impressionable at the time.'

'Wow! I had no idea you, too, were involved, Katie, what part did you play?'

Katie was about to answer when Stuart chirped in that she was a very precocious girl and nobody's fool.

'When George and I tried to recruit her to watch the house opposite, we tried to persuade her that it was a big game but she wasn't buying any of it and so we had to come clean and let her know what we had planned.'

'I think for the sake of the audience, we would all like to hear how it all started. I know we have all had the delights of hearing your adventure, but it seems you have left bits out!'

The audience shouted out their approval and so Stuart and George began to explain about the punctured ball and subsequent revenge they had planned by emptying the dog bins in the park to post through the letter box of their nemesis. At the time, he went by the name of Mr Morgan but he turned out to be someone entirely different.

'So, for everybody's benefit, they planned to post bags of dog poop through the letter box and it was Stuart who had volunteered to do the deed.'

'Bullied and coerced into it!' Stuart interjected.

'Anyway, just as he was about to shove it all through, he heard a bang and a scream from inside and, in panic, the letter box snapped shut on his fingers and as I remember the story, he ran for it, trod on some bags of dog poop and fell over, knocking himself out.'

The audience cheered and went into rapturous laughter and David Letterman took quite a while to settle them all down.

'So Katie, what went wrong?'

'From what George told me, Stuart began screaming like a girl as he ran away. Apparently, the people in the house heard him and shone a light in the garden and when Stuart saw it, he trod on the dog's muck, stupid boy!'

'Oh! Yeah! And when we went across the road to investigate, who was supposed to be looking out for us? When we didn't show up five hours later, who finally decided to do something about it? Hmm?'

'You're an exaggerating toad!'

'And you are a baggage!'

'Ha! You are a treacherous faggot!'

'Greaseball.'

'Jezebel!'

'Stinker!'

'Toerag!'

Katie said and before Stuart had a chance to respond added:;'Well, if you're going to be rude about me, I shall just ignore you!'

Having seen Stuart and Katie perform before, most of the audience clapped and cheered, knowing how the two of them bantered with each other but George and Jayne looked on in astonishment.

'I guess you don't know these two as much as you thought you did, huh, George?'

'It's not that, I didn't realise my sister had such a foul mouth.'

Dave Letterman looked perplexed.

'I don't know what Katie had said that could be deemed to be foul-mouthed.'

'Clearly you are not acquainted with what a "toerag" is?'

'I know I'm going to regret this but no, I am not acquainted with what a "toerag" is, so do please enlighten us!'

This was said with a smile since he was clearly both amused and intrigued.

'Well, in the olden days on the wooden ships, they used to fray the end of a piece of rope to make it into a rough type of brush and tow it through the water.'

'Yeeees!'

'It was tied on the end of a smaller piece of rope at one end and secured on a pole next to a box that went down to the water. The frayed end was then dangled through it.'

'YEEEEES!'

'The thing is, the box was a toilet and when the sailors had a poop, they would drag the rope up and use the frayed end to wipe their bottoms, meaning that Katie just called Stuart an arse wipe!'

He just managed to get the word 'arse' in a split second before the bleep had obscured it. (Very likely for the audience to appreciate it.) It did have the desired affect since the audience hooted with delight and Letterman decided that it went down very well and decided not to draw any attention to it.

'It would seem to me, then, that the subject of poop has a tendency to follow you around!'

Katie then chipped in by saying:

'The only reason he knows what it is, is because he uses one to shave with every morning!'

The audience clearly thought that was hilarious and began to cheer and whistle.

It took a while to settle everyone down again but then Stuart quickly chipped in:

'Poop isn't so bad. I've heard it said, "Eat poop, 60 billion flies can't be wrong!"'

'AAAAAnd on that note, I'm afraid we have overrun by a few minutes.'

The audience was in uproar with cheering and whistling and calling for more. David Letterman was trying desperately to regain control and each time he went to talk, so the noise became louder.

Eventually, the cheering subsided with David Letterman finally saying, 'Alright, alright, you win; we would love to have all four of you back again very soon. I know that Stuart and Katie are on tour but what about you, George and Jayne?'

'We are here for another two weeks and Stoopid here and Catty's tour doesn't start until we return to the UK, so if you would really like us back, we could make it in that time frame!'

'What do you say, audience? Would you like them to come back as a foursome?'

A huge cheer went up with hooting and cheering as they clapped them off the stage while David Letterman closed his show.

'Well, you have certainly come out of your sensible shell, George; I mean "Stoopid and Catty"?'

'Sorry, Bro, got caught up in the moment.'

They were ushered into a stretched limousine with fans waiting outside hoping to catch a glimpse or, better still, get an autograph.

Once home, the phone rang, and it was Stuart's agent who had said that David Letterman had asked if they could make it the following evening.

Stuart said that he was OK with it, but would need to ask if the O'Rourkes were prepared to go again so soon. Since George was still high on how the evening had been, he agreed, but Jayne seemed a little reserved. A pleading look from the other three persuaded her to agree and so it was arranged.

The hotel was one of the most expensive places George and Jayne had ever been in and had every amenity imaginable. It was extremely spacious with three huge 'en suite' bedrooms and comfortable in the extreme. All four of them were totally exhausted and hungry but feeling very satisfied.

Chapter 4

Murky and Ingrid had booked the first week of their holiday in The Swan Hotel and Spa Windermere which is right by Lake Windermere. The surroundings were beautiful and after booking in and settling in their rooms, they went to the bar for a drink and a meal. They had a leisurely supper and after a good bottle of red wine, they ventured back to their room and just as Inky was about to turn the bed down, she looked around to see Murky on his knees.

'What are you doing?' she asked excitedly.

'Look under the pillow, poppet, and don't keep me hanging!'

He had a huge smile on his face as Inky took the little box from under the pillow and saw the look of delight on her face as she opened it to expose a beautiful diamond ring.

They both chatted excitedly about the engagement and they knew both Inky's and Murky's family would like an official engagement party, but the question was where? Finally, it was decided that, since Inky's parents had never been to England, they would invite them over to the UK, where the wedding was to be held, but that was a decision for another time.

They just cuddled up and chatted until, in the early hours, they fell asleep.

The following morning, Inky was just coming to and as she slowly opened her eyes, she saw Murky's face just gazing at her. After all the excitement of the night before, which still felt so surreal because she knew that although Murky had planned to propose, it still took her by a very pleasant surprise.

Ingrid was a very attractive girl with high cheekbones accentuating her lovely eyes. She was always dressed very smartly, and her choice of clothes managed to highlight what a magnificent figure she had. In fact, it was her legs that first attracted Murky to her and when he gazed into her eyes, he was totally besotted with her. For Ingrid's part, she found him to be rather stuffy and arrogant. As Murky explained to her later, he behaved that way because he thought Ingrid was utterly gorgeous, making him feel nervous. It was a turn of fate that had brought them both together. Murky was in Poland at a NATO conference, and in the evening a banquet was laid on to which wives were invited. Ingrid's brother Konrad, who was a colonel in the Polish Army, was expected to attend despite his wife being in hospital about to give birth to their second child and since it was deemed expedient to bring a plus one, he invited his younger sister instead. He and Murky had been assigned to each other for the conference which had lasted for four days and they had become very friendly. Murky, being fluent in nearly all of the European languages, fitted in very well and became accepted by most of the delegates. At the end of the evening, Konrad was requested to remain in the city to discuss some matters concerning his next deployment and, as a result, he asked Murky if he would take Ingrid home. At first, she baulked against the idea but realising she lived a good two-hour drive away, she reluctantly accepted. As she got into the car, she made it quite plain that she found the whole thing distasteful in the extreme. She barely passed any conversation with him until eventually he made it plain that either she helped him get her home, or they would be driving all night, and he threatened to take her to the nearest train station and leave her there.

'You wouldn't dare!' she exclaimed.

By this time, Murky had had enough. she had almost been to the point of rudeness all evening and so he stopped the car and said that she was right, he wouldn't take her to a station so she could get out now.

Ingrid just looked at him and Murky felt the look on her face was so amusing, he found it difficult not to laugh but as they stared at each other, they both burst out laughing.

The atmosphere in the car on the rest of the way to Ingrid's house was far more relaxed where they both laughed a lot and found they had a great deal in common. Once at Ingrid's house, she invited him in for coffee, which he accepted, where they spent several hours talking and when Murky went to leave, he asked if he could see her again and from there the romance blossomed.

It became full-blown love for Murky when they went swimming and, being a legs man, he saw for the first time just what a tremendous figure she had and a pair of legs that he couldn't avert his eyes from.

They just lay there talking for a while and laughing as they remembered their first encounter together and making plans for their future because Murky was approaching the end of his term in the SAS. With demob just literally weeks away, that was providing the current situation was brought to a conclusion in time, neither was sure, what they were going to do. Neither liked the seclusion of the countryside or the hubbub of a city but would much prefer to live in a town. Murky was more than willing to move to Poland but Ingrid really wanted to move to the UK because in her current job, although it was reasonably well paid, she felt the prospects in England were far better.

The four agents assigned to watch out for them were as good as Major Bradley's word and, by all appearances, they didn't even acknowledge each other, other than to pass a polite greeting as they either passed in the hallway or if they saw each other in the dining room. There were two couples, one sharing a room next door to theirs and the other just a few rooms down on the opposite side of the corridor. Although not romantically attached, they were both highly trained professionals who would take turns to sleep through the night while the other kept a watching vigil. Secret cameras were positioned watching Murky's door and along the corridor, while another was rigged up watching outside his window and the street below and, although they were on the second floor, no chances were being taken.

They took their time getting ready for breakfast and had planned a leisurely day ahead. Murky suggested they should try to hire a small boat for a leisurely trip around one of the lakes and then find a nice pub to have lunch.

The weather was beautiful with lots of sunshine and just a refreshingly gentle breeze.

It was essential for Murky to keep the team designated to keep them safe and informed, and so he had a secure phone which he used to contact Major Bradley's office and it would then be relayed to the team.

Whenever they went anywhere, one of the couples, knowing Murky's plans, would arrange to be somewhere in the same vicinity, while the other couple would split in two with one staying in one room while the other would keep watch from the other.

Murky and Ingrid were enjoying a lovely, sedate motor around the lake with just enough wind to keep the atmosphere pleasantly cool while not disturbing the water and making it uncomfortable. Their two minders were not far away in another motor launch.

Once they had had enough, they went in search of a pub and again, the minders were not far away, sitting by a window while Murky and Ingrid sat and ate in the garden. All the time they were being kept safe, the team would have one eye on Murky while, at the same time, looking around for anything that might appear suspicious.

As it turned out, it was quite an uneventful and pleasant afternoon. Once lunch was finished, they got back into the car and returned to the hotel closely followed by the team.

Wherever they went, whether in strange or familiar surroundings, they were always alert to anything that didn't look right. Even Murky, despite being relaxed and knowing he had good backup, was always alert, and on their return to the hotel, Murky's sixth sense began to niggle at him. He had no idea why and felt it might just be nerves and not enough to report to the team.

As was agreed, the team ventured to their rooms and used a coded knock to let the occupant know they were back, when just to the right of the girl's head, a hole appeared in the door splintering a large 'shake' surrounding the small hole. The man grabbed his female team member and they ran along the corridor to warn Murky and Ingrid.

'What's wrong, has our cover been blown?' Murky asked.

'Stella just knocked her door and waited for Mark to return the coded knock but someone in the room used a gun with a silencer shooting through the door. It just missed Stella's head so we came straight to get you and we have to get away. We need to contact Major Bradley to call this in. I have to assume that my partner Janet and also Mark have either been compromised, but knowing the way these people have operated in the past, we may have to come to terms with the fact that they are most likely both dead!'

There was no sign of the concierge or any of the staff, but they had no time to try and find them.

They decided that the best way to get out of the hotel was to keep well away from the entrance and find a different escape route through either the kitchen or some other less conspicuous exit. They carefully moved forward with their senses highly tuned in on the surrounding noises and listening for any changes, no matter how slight.

During all this time, Ingrid remained remarkably calm; every time Murky looked behind to reassure her, she always mouthed that she was fine, giving him a smile. He was so proud of her: where many other women would either panic or at least look frightened, here was Ingrid looking like she was on a big adventure.

Because Murky, being on holiday, obviously didn't carry any weapons, he and Ingrid walked between Alec and Stella who were naturally both armed. Alec cautiously crept out of the laundry exit and indicated that it was clear.

Outside there was very little cover and so he suggested he stay and keep watch while the three of them made their escape and Alec would keep them covered.

Just as they were about to make a break for it, in the distance was the unmistakeable sound of sirens and the thumping of helicopter blades; someone in the hotel must have managed to raise the alarm, and within minutes, the helicopter was hovering and scouring the area with an armed police officer clearly visible by the cockpit door.

As they waited, Alec was watching their front while Stella was poised with her gun at the ready to make sure that they weren't about to be attacked from behind.

'Bloody hell, Murky, those bastards are really out to get you, I wonder how on earth they knew where you were?'

Murky suddenly went very cold and Ingrid, noticing his sudden change, asked what was wrong.

'The only other people outside of the office and the six of us who knew our whereabouts were my parents, and if I'm right about being followed on the way to Stansted Airport…'

He didn't finish his sentence and immediately reached for his phone and rang their number. There was no reply and in panic, thinking he might have misdialled, he tried again.

'Oh my God! I hope they haven't been…'

He didn't want to use the words that they may have been killed or even worse, tortured and killed and his mind went into overdrive when he almost jumped out of his skin when his mobile rang.

'Hello, darling, sorry we didn't get to the phone in time, Dad and I were enjoying a gin and tonic in the garden. What did you want?'

Murky almost wept with relief knowing that they were safe.

'Mum, has anyone been to see you recently since I came to lunch the other day.'

'Actually yes, a charming young man was here the day before yesterday and said he was a friend of yours from the Army and wanted to get in touch for old times' sake. He was very nice and stayed for a cup of tea and a biscuit and we had a lovely chat. It was very strange, though: he didn't remember Ben or George or even Jonah for that matter, and when I mentioned it, he said that you both served together years ago and I assumed it was before you went into your special job.'

'Did you tell him where we were going on holiday?'

'He didn't ask at first but the conversation really revolved around what you were doing now and had you left the Army yet. I told him you were thinking about it, but would decide when you came back from your holiday.'

'And then he asked you where I was?'

'Well, yes, darling, why?'

'Mum, I need you to listen very carefully, I want you to lock all the doors and don't answer any phone calls or open the door to anyone. I'm going to get someone round who will knock on the door twice, pause, knock three more times a bit faster, and then twice more. Have you got that, Mum? It's very important.'

'Oh dear, this does sound very exciting and "cloak-and-dagger".'

'Mum, have you got what I have just asked you to do?'

'Yes, darling, but what is this all about? I'm sure you're overreacting, and everything will be fine!'

'*MUM! YOU REALLY HAVE TO LISTEN TO ME*, I haven't got time to explain, now please read that all back to me.'

Since Murky sounded so urgent, his mother read his instructions back and he told her he would contact her later. He then instantly spoke to Major Bradley on his secure line and requested that a team be despatched to his family because they now needed to be kept safe.

'I really can't afford for my parents to be used as a weapon against me, sir, and, although it seems as though George and I are a definite target and even that aside, I also feel we're all fairly sure that they are targeting London again.'

'I agree, Murky, and I will get someone over to your parents' house right away.'

Major Bradley rang the nearest police station and explained the possible dangers their officers could be facing and promised armed backup units within the next twenty minutes.

In fact, it was the armed units who arrived first as a helicopter arrived and began despatching operatives as they abseiled directly around Murky's parents' house. One went to the front door and used the coded knock and was relieved when Murky's mother answered the door and the whole area was secured. The police arrived moments later and once they established there was nothing they could do to help, they were stood down and returned to their station.

Murky was immediately informed that his parents were safe and so carried on looking into the attack that had occurred from within one of their rooms.

The armed unit had gone through the hotel and declared it clear and that it appeared that the assassin had made his or her escape. They confirmed that Mark was indeed dead, but it was Janet who had called in and raised the alarm. She had been observing the cameras along the hall and saw someone suspicious lurking around Mark and Stella's room and he had managed to obtain a door key and let himself in. It was just a few moments later when Murky, Ingrid and the two bodyguards arrived and, realising an emergency was occurring, she called it in.

The concierge was in fact dead along with some of the other members of staff but most had managed to escape and on realising it was safe to return, they gradually went back to the hotel. There they were interviewed by the police in order to try and establish what they all knew about the attack.

Some were reasonably calm but others were clearly distressed and in shock.

It seems that it was a lone male assassin who clearly wanted to get in and out as soon as possible, otherwise the survivors would have certainly been hunted down and killed. If Murky hadn't returned when he had, it could have had an entirely different outcome because from what Janet had said, the attack had only just started a short while earlier.

It was a shame that the holiday Murky had planned to spend with Ingrid was now in tatters and it did leave him in a quandary.

Should he send her home where she would be safe? Or would

that be putting her in more danger since these unknown assailants seemed to have no problem negotiating any foreign borders?

It was Charles Bradley who eventually came up with a possible solution.

'The best way to keep Ingrid safe is to let the two of you share a married quarter inside the camp. I know it isn't ideal, my boy, but at least the camp is guarded and patrolled by sentries and dogs. You will both be safe there and can almost live like a married couple, but I doubt that poor Ingrid will take to being kept almost like a prisoner. If you explain to her that it is a matter of national security, that whoever is responsible for all this carnage cannot be allowed to capture her and compromise your ability to function!'

'I didn't know that we had married quarters in the camp, sir!'

'They don't officially exist, Sergeant Major, but bearing in mind the kind of work that we do, it is sometimes necessary to protect families in situations such as this. There are shops, a cinema and most of the comforts of home and again, I admit, not ideal, but once we get to the bottom of what Okorie is up to and we are able to neutralise him, I'm afraid it is the only way.'

Murky reluctantly nodded his head in agreement and was about to leave the room when the major said, 'By the way, Murky, your family have been airlifted by helicopter and flown to a secret location where they will be kept safe while we try to get this bloody mess sorted out.'

Chapter 5

It was getting near the time for Stuart, Katie and the O'Rourkes to be collected and taken to the studio to begin their second session with David Letterman, and, although it seemed like a good idea at the time, George was beginning to feel apprehensive while Stuart and Katie seemed to take it in their stride.

Stuart looked across at George and noticed his agitation and told him not to worry, he said that both he and Katie still got nervous before appearing, but after making so many public appearances, they were more able to keep the nerves under control.

'When we first started out in America and not knowing how well we were going to be received by the audience, I was physically sick just minutes before I went on. After a while, Katie was invited to join me so the audience could see what this poor, long-suffering woman was like. Since then, she has been appearing with me on every show, but before Katie was to appear for the first time, she looked like a 'slowworm' that had overdosed on speed. She couldn't stop shaking and by shaking, I mean, well, if I got the shakes that bad and went to the toilet for a wee, I would have had to have gone into a cubicle because anyone watching would have either thought I was masturbating or trying to pull it off!'

This light-hearted take did make George laugh and Jayne was trying hard to hide her amusement, but Katie just looked across at

Stuart and gave him one of 'those' looks.

'You are gross, Stuart Baxter!' she said.

'It's your fault, Katie, I didn't even know what the expression 'bloody hell' meant before I met you: you have completely corrupted me!'

Before Katie was able to answer, they were all called forward into the studio where they were met with a rapturous applause as they were ushered in to take their seats.

As was always the case whenever the Baxters appeared; it took David Letterman several minutes to calm the audience down but eventually they settled down eagerly waiting for the interview to begin.

'As I recall as you left last time, you were talking a great deal about your experiences, but as I understand it, you, Stuart with George and your other good friend Ben got up to a lot of mischief in your neighbourhood where sometimes the police would knock on your parents' doors asking where you had all been the night before?'

Stuart and George just sat there for a moment and just as they were about to answer, David Letterman realised that he had been told what had happened to Ben and promptly apologised and said he hoped he hadn't caused any distress.

It was George who answered by saying that the three of them always liked to play tricks and jokes on people which was never intended to be malicious.

'But I do know that our parents were sometimes driven to distraction by some of the things that we used to do but I feel that it's something we would rather not talk about at the moment; it reminds us of…of…o.'

Jayne moved over to comfort him and it was Stuart who decided to lighten the mood.

'Pay no attention, folks, he's trying to milk it: he always does this when he isn't getting any laughs!'

At first the audience weren't sure whether or not to laugh but George very quickly took control of his emotions and looked at Stuart and said, 'Oh heck, Jayne, I've been rumbled, that's typical of you, young Baxter, you have been the same ever since you discovered

Father Christmas wasn't who you thought he was!'

David Letterman quickly picked up on this and asked what it was about.

'For the benefit of all the children everywhere, the real Father Christmas was very, very busy one year and asked Stuart's dad if he could help him out. Not being used to doing this, he got very drunk and fell down the stairs, waking Stuart up who burst into tears and thought that the real Father Christmas didn't want to bring him any presents!'

Katie then chipped in by saying he cried like a little baby.

'I was at a very tender age and it broke my heart: how could you remind me of such a traumatic time?'

'Stuart, you were eighteen years old!'

'It's not my fault my parents were good at keeping secrets!'

By this time the audience had cottoned on that it was a big wind-up and began to laugh and the mood became a good deal lighter with George's earlier discomfort being forgotten.

'So, George and Jayne, what plans do you have for when you get back home?'

'Well, since we still have a while to go yet with these two horrors, and putting aside for a moment that you have just "Joyced" us, it's back to work for both of us.'

'OK, I'll buy it … "Joyced"?'

'It's my mother's name and every time I went home on leave, the first thing she would say was: "When are you going back?"'

'Ah, I see; and you both work in the education system: is it something you enjoy?'

'The children are lovely and if you are fair with them, they aren't so disruptive. Don't get me wrong, they can be little horrors but I love them all the same.'

The audience had been chuckling all the time that George was talking and on looking across at Stuart and Katie, they could see they were miming and imitating George and pulling silly faces and using exaggerated hand movements.

'Are they always like this with you two, I mean, are they ever not messing around?'

George explained that since he had known both of them pretty much all his life, he had grown used to them.

'I feel I'm OK talking about our younger days with Ben now. I wasn't expecting it when you mentioned it earlier and it did catch me unawares but the three of us, that is Ben, Stuart and I, would very often be in one fix or another. Normally, it was the three of us who would get into trouble with the adults around the area but we were well known and our mischief was never offensive. However, being the biggest and stockiest of the three of us when Ben and Stuart picked a fight with some other boys, once things started to look like it would end in a punch-up, they would both rely on me to get them out of trouble.'

'So, you would protect them despite bringing most of their troubles on themselves?'

'The thing is, Ben was a wiry little guy and could look after himself, but being the smallest of the three of us, he would normally try to bite off more than he could chew.'

'And what about Stuart, did he like to get in the mix of it with Ben?'

'No comment other than to say, more often than not, he was able quite a lot of the time to lower the tension by using his best weapon. He has always had the ability to have people in fits of laughter because he is a naturally funny person.' He would really only get involved in a real fight if he was pushed into a corner, but most times it was avoided because if his humour didn't get him out of trouble, he had me as his backup. It was rare, though.'

'So, Stuart, tell us more about your friendship with George and Ben?'

'Apart from what George has said, there is nothing to add: all we did was to get up to mischief, although I will say that the gorgeous prima donna George over there who was sitting preening himself just now, making out he was our big saviour, can also be treacherous! Last year when he came home for two weeks' leave for one of our friends' stag weekend and wedding, one of the things we did was to go paintballing. There were several games but the last one was hunt the stag where the groom and best man are given the count of ten to run for cover before the rest of the group open fire. I was the poor best man who had to run for it with the groom but on the count of one, our dear friend and saviour started firing directly at me. Within two seconds, I got four shots in the back, three in the butt, two on one cheek, and one on the other and as I turned to get revenge, I got another three in the chest. I was black and blue all over and when I got home, Katie thought that I had either been mugged or raped!'

'Think yourself lucky that I ran out of ammunition when I did, otherwise you would have looked more like a clownfish!'

Katie then chirped in with a perfect rendition of Oprah Winfrey followed by Gwyneth Paltrow and Natalie Portman in a mock admonishment of the two men as if they were naughty boys and she was either their mother, wife or auntie.

The audience were stunned by her performance and gave her a standing ovation. Katie had always known she had a talent for mimicking celebrities and had been practising to perfect it all the time she and Stuart had been in England.

David Letterman was completely taken aback and asked why she had never done something like that before.

'I've known you two for several years and never knew you could do impersonations!'

Stuart said, 'She has always done it and it's great for me because it's like going to bed with a different woman every night, but I hate Tuesdays, though!'

'Well, I know I need to know and I'm sure so does the audience: why do you hate Tuesdays?'

'Because that's when she does Donald Trump!'

At this point, even Letterman, a veteran of hosting chat shows, found himself unable to speak and the audience were on the point of being hysterical.

Once David Letterman managed to salvage a modicum of self-control, he announced that he needed to bring his next guest on and asked if the four of them would stay to the end and they agreed.

David Letterman's next guest was Harrison Ford who had heard all about Stuart and George's escapades and said he was delighted to meet two real life Indiana Joneses. Katie and Jayne were just sitting there gazing up at him with adoring eyes. Harrison just looked back, giving them a cheeky wink.

A lot of the interview started with Harrison's next film and so the evening progressed, but really it was Stuart who kept chipping in making everyone laugh.

After about half an hour, David Letterman heard something in his earpiece and briefly left the studio.

When he re-entered, he looked a bit confused but interrupted his five guests and said to the Baxters and O'Rourkes that some people were outside the studio and needed to speak to them urgently.

The audience gave them a standing ovation and cheered as they left and clapped for a good few minutes once they had departed. They were met by a surly-looking gentleman who politely requested they follow him and led them to a room which was occupied by two tough-looking men. It was clear by their appearance that they both had something to do with security because of the black suits and inevitable earpieces.

'Good evening to you all, I am Jonathon Taylor and this is my colleague Leroy Jones. I am sure you must all be very confused, and I apologise for ruining your evening, but a Major Charles Bradley from UK intelligence has contacted the CIA offices. He has requested that we take you to somewhere safe because there has been an attempt on a certain Sergeant Major Murphy's life, and it is believed that you four could also be in danger!'

George went cold and was trying to make sense of what he was hearing.

'Do we know why or who? I mean in the work we used to do together; it could be any number of possible suspects.'

'I'm afraid we don't have that information but when you are taken from here, and don't worry, it isn't what we call protective custody but to a penthouse suite at a hotel, you will all be kept safe. As I understand it, Major Bradley is being flown out as we speak to brief you tomorrow afternoon.'

They were then ushered away to an awaiting car where they were taken to a military establishment and flown to Reagan Airport. A stretch limousine was on the runway to collect them with four men who, by their appearance, were bodyguards, all wearing dark suits and dark glasses with the inevitable wire emanating from an ear. Once embarked, the limousine left with two other cars with the limo in between.

'Bloody hell, George!'

George said that if Stuart mentioned the ball not being worth it, he would give him a severe beating. He was trying to lighten the mood since it was a huge comedown from the elation at being on the Late Show with David Letterman.

'How can you be so relaxed about it? I mean, what the heck is going on?'

'I'm not sure, Stoopot, but I think I have an idea that it could be something to do with the incident a couple of years ago when someone tried to bump me off: they nearly succeeded, too!'

I'll be seeing the major later and I'll let you know when I find out. I don't think anyone is specifically out to get you, old mate, but they might try to get at me through you two because you are my best friend and Katie is my sister.'

Katie suddenly took in a deep breath and exclaimed:

'What about little Georgie? He's still in our hotel with his nannie!'

The guard sitting in the back alongside the pair explained that there was no cause for concern because their son, complete with nannie, were safely ensconced in the suite and both were waiting for them.

There was a huge sigh of relief and they arrived at the hotel without any incidents.

Once settled, they did their best to occupy their minds. none of them had an appetite and Jayne in particular, was visibly shaken because in her heart she knew it was most likely connected to the incident of a couple of years ago.

It was a restless night for all of them despite the suite being luxurious and exceptionally comfortable.

The following morning, they waited nervously until Charles Bradley got in touch with them.

'Do you think that you will be asked to go back to the UK, George?'

'I'm not sure, Jayne poppet, the thing is I am still on the Reserve List and could be called up if it was ever deemed necessary. The thing is, we could sit here pondering what might or might not happen and it will be better for us if we changed the subject until we hear from the major.'

It was at two-thirty in the afternoon when there was a knock at the door and it was Charles Bradley who had finally come to brief them.

Once all the introductions had been made, he tried his best to put them at their ease.

'Since this is likely to be a military briefing, would you like Katie, Nannie and me to leave you all to it?'

Charles Bradley explained that it would be in their interest to remain and listen to what he had to say.

'It would seem that there is some kind of resurgence of the Urban Commandos and the man behind it is a gentleman named Adwin Okorie who is the older brother of Afolabi Okorie. The two brothers were the youngest of a family of five other boys. The older ones used to bully the two youngsters and by the time they were thirteen, the three older brothers were mysteriously bumped off. Apparently, the mother and father were terrified of the two of them and left them to their own devices. They proved to be born survivors and both were vicious. in fact, Adwin is more evil than Afolabi was.'

'Now as far as we know, Adwin has been active in the area of deep-sea diving and he has been hiring a group of experts to train his trusted aids in the discipline. Intelligence is fairly sparse because whenever an attempt has been made to infiltrate the group, it seems they are discovered within twenty-four hours and murdered. In fact, three operatives managed to get into the group a short while ago, but within hours, they were found floating down the Thames and all had been executed. We had hopes there might have been a breakthrough because two of the men were from UK intelligence and the third a Ghanaian Special Forces major. Britain have been working closely with the Ghanaian authorities since the debacle of two years ago and both authorities are beginning to wonder whether or not there is a leak in either one or both of our agencies.

'So where does that leave the four of us?' asked George.

'I have spoken to the American authorities and we jointly agree that it would be best for you and Jayne to return to the UK. As for Stuart and his family, I have been assured that they will be carefully looked after and it is felt that without you here, there is less chance any attempt would be made to get to you through them. They will both therefore be able to continue with their tour albeit under the watchful eye of the American authorities. As for the two of you, I'm afraid that because of your knowledge and experience of this group George, you are returning to active duty. Jayne, I think you will appreciate that you leading a normal life while this is going on could really blow the whole thing out of the water. If you were ever taken, you would be used to influence George for their own ends and so we are afraid that we must insist on keeping you out of the way for the time being. Believe me, Jayne, they would not hesitate to really hurt you while they film it and likely put on social media and we can't afford to have George influenced in this manner. Murky and his fiancée are currently ensconced in an Army facility where you will all be based for the time being. Trust me, as bad as it all seems, this group is particularly corrosive and showing mercy is so far away from the diving board that there is no water for miles around, so to speak. I discovered that you both now work in the same school and the headteacher and Chairman of Governors have been informed and they wish you both well.'

'So, what happens now, when do we fly back?'

'I'm staying here this evening and you will be flying back with me in the morning. In the meantime, I have a table ready for us all to have a meal later which, as you would imagine, is out of the public eye. Stuart and Katie, because of their popularity, would draw unwanted publicity to us all and we will therefore be incognito. 'I am happy to say that despite the moratorium on hospitality, I am permitted to let HM Government foot the bill. I will come for you at about seven, would that be alright?'

It was agreed and Charles left, leaving the four of them to digest all that they had heard.

The meal was a superb spread and no expense spared. even little Georgie and Nanny were invited, and they talked about everything and nothing and were at pains not to discuss anything remotely related to recent events.

The following morning, just as George and Jayne were about to leave, Katie asked if it would be alright to see them off at the airport. This did cause a bit of a stir since it meant extra security but after a short time, everything was organised and once Nanny and Little Georgie were in a secure place, they set off in the same car with two other cars in convoy, one in front and one behind. It was a fraught journey with a great deal of small talk to pass the time, but in the back of their minds was the prospect of George being killed or horribly injured and it was a relief when the convoy finally got to Dulles Airport. They were all ushered in but the Baxters were quickly recognised and people began to whistle and cheer. Stuart waved and shouted he was sorry but he couldn't stop to talk, and the security guards gently shepherded them through to the departure lounge where it was decided it would be best all round if they said their farewells now so that security could get Stuart and Katie back through to the cars in order to let things settle down again.

'I think that this might have been a big mistake, bro, I'm really sorry!'

Katie just burst into tears and said to her brother to be careful and hugged him, not wanting to let him go.

'I'll be fine, Katie, I promise I won't take any silly risks and I'll make sure that Jayne will keep in touch to let you know that I am 'A'

OK. Alright, poppet?'

'It's just that I felt wretched when you went out to Ghana to get Okorie, George, and hoped that when you got back safely that that would be the end to it and to see it starting all over again!!!!'

She couldn't stop sobbing and even Stuart was emotional as they were leaving the departure lounge.

While Major Bradley and the O'Rourkes waited to be called forward, the furore just a short time earlier had drawn the attention of a group that the security agency had been at pains to avoid.

Chapter 6

George and Murky greeted each other like two long-lost brothers trying to see who would win the bear-hugging contest. Since both were as strong as each other, neither was proclaimed the winner, but that was to be the last of the joviality for a while as they began discussing what needed to be done to discover the intentions of Okorie and his cronies.

There was to be a briefing in two days, not just to allow George to recover from jetlag, but also to get the rest of the team together to try and thrash out a strategy. Also, it would allow Murky, Ingrid, George and Jayne to spend a bit of quality time together since it was most likely the girls would be without seeing their partners for an unknown amount of time.

The following days were quite enjoyable and while the facilities were a little limited, they filled their time eating, drinking and chatting and, although knowing what was to happen in the following days, it was not mentioned and pushed to the backs of their minds. Ingrid and Jayne became friends immediately and ganged up on the boys.

All too soon, however, the two days were over and George and Murky were collected and driven to the briefing.

It was quite a tearful farewell because, although Jayne was able to cope with George exacting his revenge in Ghana two years before, she was filled with dread this time. Ingrid for her part appeared to be calm but inside she was naturally very anxious.

Ingrid put an arm around Jayne and said.

'Well, it's just you and me, kid, against the rest of the world!'

It was only a short journey from the barracks to MI6, and once the group was assembled, Emma Belchin began her brief.

'Well, since we last met, we have just a little more information on Okorie and the destination of the *Ardent Ventura* we believe to be UK waters. Now it might seem strange, but since Okorie hasn't been found guilty of any crime, despite knowing he is about as clean as a sewer rat, he is allowed to enter our territory. Having spoken with MI5 and MI6, we considered denying him access but on reflection, however, it was agreed that that might be a tactical error in as much we could lose sight of him. At least allowing him in, we can keep a closer eye on him. Questions?'

Nobody had any at that time and so the briefing continued, and the lights were dimmed while a PowerPoint presentation was displayed on a large screen.

Emma Belchin then asked Charles Bradley to continue.

'These are the facts as we currently know them. *Ardent Ventura* is coming to the UK but we don't know her actual destination. There is a code word they are using which is "RHYMOW". We also know that they seem to be training some of their personnel in the discipline of diving and have procured several sets of air breathing apparatus.' Also, according to information from our Ghanaian counterparts, just prior to the *Ventura* setting sail, a raid was made at a commercial explosive's depot and a large quantity of plastic explosives with detonators and fuzes were stolen. Now coincidentally at the time, Okorie was known to be in the area with most of his lieutenants and, although they were the most likely culprits, as usual, nothing could be proved. At the moment, that is all the information available so now on to our response. We are keeping the *Ventura* under close but discreet surveillance, but our problem is we have no idea how many are ashore already. We also have no idea how many Urban Commandos are involved because since the rout of two years ago, they have been relatively quiet, and we aren't sure of their numbers. Does anyone have questions?'

The room was silent as they all took in what appeared to be an impossible task. There was so little information that there didn't seem to be a viable strategy available to them.

Murky raised his hand and asked whether or not estimations could be made from what was known to be the Commandos' strength before the group was broken up two years before.

'It would be difficult if not impossible to extrapolate the information we had then to what little we know now but for those present not privy to what Sergeant Major Murphy is referring, when the last attack was foiled, it became clear that we had a corrupt Minister called Julien Algar who was being made very rich by giving Afolabi Okorie secret information. He was very close to the Commandos and he knew everything that was being planned. He was disgraced and lucky not to be tried for treason. In exchange for giving the authorities all the information that he had, his sentence was reduced from 25 years to ten.'

'Are we certain that there have been no surreptitious attempts to make contact with him?'

'I doubt it very much, George, since being devoid of any Cabinet knowledge, he has become low-value as a source of information to them, so that begs the question: what do we need to do? I think that now would be a good time for a comfort break because tea and biscuits are due any minute and so we shall adjourn for twenty minutes.'

During the break, George was deep in thought and Murky asked what was wrong, but all George would say was that he had a bad feeling that his sister, Georgie and Stuart might be in danger.

'I can't explain it, Murks, but my mind has been in overdrive since we left America and while I sometimes feel I have a sixth sense about something affecting me directly, this feels a bit different. Probably my imagination, my man; we'd best get back to the briefing.'

Once back in the briefing, they were all informed that they were to be joined by a person from the Ghanaian Special Forces called

Chizoba Katlego who had been invited to train with the current team once they knew what likely eventuality Okorie was planning. Chizoba was also an expert in diving and had been decorated for his bravery in tackling a guerrilla faction from almost sinking a frigate. He had nearly lost his life because his airline had been cut but even with a limited amount of oxygen in his lungs, he managed to overcome his assailant.

Major Bradley began to summarise what had been previously discussed when the door was opened and a tall, dark-haired gentleman entered. He introduced himself as Chizoba and was asked if he would like to take a seat. Once all the introductions had taken place, Major Bradley recapped on all the information that had been discussed before Chizoba's arrival. He was very well built and had a strong face with deep jowls. Although he was affable, there was a hardness about him and a supreme air of confidence.

When Major Bradley finished going over the briefing, he said that he wanted to set the group into two teams, even though at this moment in time, there was little to go on.

'Since Jeremy, Steve and Chizoba are experts in underwater operations, I would like to put you three together as Team Maritime and George, Murky and Brendan, you will be known as Team Land. Both teams will liaise closely together and in order to help you gel together, we'll devise some joint exercises that will gear you up for any eventuality. Any questions?'

Brendan raised his hand and asked if they could talk about the code word.

'If it is an acronym, it seems to be a little lengthy and may I ask Chizoba whether there would be words in his native tongue that might give a clue as to what each of the letters could possibly stand for.'

Chizoba shrugged and said that he wasn't able to match any of the letters that could shine any light on its meaning.

'You clearly have something on your mind, Brendan, care to air it?'

'I might be putting two and two together and making five, but could it also be R-I-M-O? With all the emphasis by Okorie regarding diving etc.; could the target possibly be the *Richard Montgomery*?'

Murky said he had never heard of him and asked why he would be a target.

'It's not a 'he', it's a 'she'. She was an American Liberty ship built during World War II, one of the 2,710 used to carry cargo during the war. The ship was wrecked off the Nore sandbank in the Thames Estuary and she is full of live ordnance.'

Murky laughed and said that his ignorance of the ship stays in this room.

'The thing is, there is an exclusion zone around the ship and each year, divers are sent down to see how all the explosives are decaying and always the answer is the same: they are still in a volatile state and still leeching nitroglycerine into the sea at Southend-on-Sea. In fact, you can see her masts at low tide from the shore. Should the ammunition suddenly erupt, it could send a tidal surge along the Thames right into the heart of the capital, not to mention all the destruction that it would cause on the way. As an aside, I wouldn't recommend eating any shell food from the area!'

'Thank you, Brendan, that does make a lot of sense and now you have put it that way, I think we can assume to know what the target is. The way forward as I see it is that Team Maritime join in with the discreet surveillance and we'll Heli Lift you three on-board HMS *Piebald* complete with all your equipment and weapons. As for Team Land, once we've devised a training programme that befits the suspected operation, we'll send you to Southend-on-Sea to a 'hotel where you can set up a surveillance!'

'Won't it look a bit suspicious with three men staying long-term in the hotel?'

'We would like to get some female backup in there with you, but at this moment in time, I don't think it would serve any real purpose.'

Murky suggested that perhaps one male stay in the hotel while the other two remain in hired dwellings not far from Southend-on-Sea such as Great Wakering.

'I know the area well and should the hotel team require assistance, we could be there in minutes. That way, all the time it is quiet, two men could stay in the digs and rotate the surveillance on a monthly basis. It would not raise suspicion with any guests because there is a relatively quick turnover. We could let the proprietors know that there is a scheme to see the viability to increase crop yields on Foulness Island.'

'That seems a good idea, Murky, I think there's a reasonable hotel right on the seafront and the *Richard Montgomery* can be seen from there. I'm not entirely sure of the name but it has a red frontage to it!'

'It's called the Roslin, sir, and very hospitable. The food is excellent, too!'

Major Bradley thought for a moment and suggested that it wouldn't look right for any of them to be ensconced in the Roslin all day.

'No, sir, because there is an MoD establishment onsite on Foulness Island, I'm sure we can persuade the authorities to allow us an office no matter how small as long as it can accommodate three people and has a phone and computer. There are things we can do whilst in there in planning and mind mapping our response without letting on too much about our mission. We may also need to enhance our bomb disposal skills: that way we can counter any possible outcome.'

'Well, I think that now at least we have a plan, as obscure as it is, and since that is all we have to go on, I think we should execute immediately. Good day and thank you all.'

Chapter 7

The American population tuning in on the early morning NEWS were shocked to see a slaughter just outside the residence of a very popular and well-known British family.

Stuart and Katie Baxter were about to alight from their car with their nanny and son Georgie when gunmen attacked the security contingent protecting them.

The story was breaking on every news channel and people were watching in utter disbelief as the story was unfolding.

Both Stuart and Katie had been bundled into a car which left at speed and the whereabouts of their young son and nanny were at this time unknown.

Luckily, the public had responded rapidly and a police helicopter had been despatched while a neighbour had quickly jumped in his car and was following the apparent kidnappers. He was giving instructions on which direction the perpetrators were heading. Within a short time, there were several police vehicles closing in and so the chase was underway.

There had been a great deal of speculation surrounding the couple when during their last appearance on David Letterman's Late Show they were suddenly ushered off. Since then, the Baxters had limited their appearances and were watched closely by the US security agency. Interviews with Letterman didn't reveal much information mainly because he didn't know why they left the studio so quickly and why they were not seen as often.

The American public were beginning to have a good idea as to why their behaviour had changed so dramatically and now, they were in outrage because they had taken the Baxters into their bosoms and loved them as they would family.

It wasn't difficult for the public to see the direction of the chase because it was getting up-to-date coverage on the television. Many people got into their cars to try and help, but in the end, the police had to put out a bulletin ordering them to return home since they were hampering the chase.

Finally, the police managed to herd the car down a long road where there were only three means of exiting, and at each of the three roads, there were police armed with stingers that would be rolled out in front of the car to burst the tyres. There were SWAT teams at every position, and they had been given strict orders to shoot and wound only. They wanted at least one of them alive for questioning.

The chase ended almost as abruptly as it had begun when the car, on striking the stingers, began to slew wildly across the road, just missing a water hydrant and finally coming to a halt.

Before anyone in the car had time to react, the SWAT teams were straight at the car shouting at the occupants to show their hands clearly but one of the kidnappers went for his gun and his head disappeared into a bright red stain on the rest of the occupants. There were two other people remaining in the car other than the Baxters and they immediately raised their hands and were bundled unceremoniously out of the car. They were forced to the ground and cuffed and swiftly taken into the protective custody of a police vehicle because by now, an avenging mob were beginning to gather and had to be retrained where shots were fired into the air by the SWAT team to try and restore order.

A short while later, the Baxters were seen to be getting out of the car and, although they were clearly shaken, they both managed to wave and smile at the crowd with some of them shouting how were they feeling? Stuart shouted back, 'Well, at least that has given us some more material to work on. As soon as I find out who they are, they're getting a bill for dry-cleaning!'

The crowd cheered and wished them well.

As they got into a car, they were informed that Nanny and Georgie were safe because a quick-thinking neighbour had seen what was happening and rushed them into their house for safety.

On the way to their home, Katie suddenly began shaking and sobbing as the circumstances began to hit home. Stuart put his arm around her and tried to comfort her, but she said she didn't want to tour America anymore.

'We could have lost Georgie, Stuart, he could have been killed!'

She then cried uncontrollably but Stuart talked quietly to her and suggested that that wasn't going to happen.

'The thing is, poppet, the chances of it ever happening again are remote mainly because the American authorities will be watching us ever more closely and also because this attempt was such a mammoth failure due to the response of the American public. They would be unwise to try again. It is very important that we show ourselves in public as soon as possible, my darling, to show we are not frightened and won't be intimidated.'

'But the man who got shot, Stuart, was horrible. I've never seen such a horrible thing and never want to again!'

'I have seen worse things than that in Africa when George and I were kidnapped and believe me, after a while, the memory begins to fade but we have to carry on, sweet. The Americans have shown us a lot of affection and I don't want to offend them by what would appear to be that we're running away and deserting them. I'm going to contact our agent in the next few days and ask if we could be invited on the Late Show with David Letterman and we are going to discuss between us how to turn this into a big joke.'

The rest of the journey home was in silence.

Naturally, the press wanted an interview but Stuart sent a message through his agent to ask for a bit of respite since the experience had been quite traumatic but promised if they left them alone, both he and Katie would oblige them.

Once they were reunited with Georgie, they sat down and tried to relax, and a very short time later, a counsellor who was an expert in helping where a stressful situation had occurred, was let in by security and began talking to them both.

The counsellor was called Laura and spoke quietly in a delightful and reassuring way. She had an Irish accent and both Stuart and Katie were immediately put at their ease.

She asked Katie first what she wanted and had she been able to at least settle her nerves at all?

Katie was still clearly very shaken but after she and Stuart had removed their soiled clothes and showered, she said she had been feeling a little better. She had had a small gin and tonic but explained it wasn't so much the attempt to kidnap them that bothered her so much, but more the sight of a head suddenly disappearing into a bright red ball.

Stuart suddenly began to giggle and broke out into an uncontrollable laugh. It was partly caused by nerves, but the way Katie had described the disappearing head.

She looked sourly at Stuart and said that it wasn't funny, Stuart.

'I have never had you down as a sick-minded person, but it was horrible!'

'Katie, my darling girl, firstly, I'm not denying it was horrible but whoever it was deserved to get killed. As for the other two, they may well rot for years in an American correctional centre but not before they give the authorities as much information as is useful. Secondly, my darling, this failed attempt is likely to keep George and Murky a lot safer but what has made me laugh is the way you described the head. I am going to think about that, and we *will* be using it when we are back with Letterman!'

Laura had let them both talk without interrupting them until finally asking Stuart why he seemed not to have been badly affected by the ordeal.

'The thing is, Laura, I'm not sure if you know, but when Katie's brother George and I were young boys, we were kidnapped by an arms-smuggling gang and whisked off to Africa. Two of the group were psychopathic murderers and it was their leader who kept us safe. He had several pseudonyms but turned out to be a West German intelligence officer called Bernhardt von Austerlitz who had infiltrated the group. The two henchmen were called Jürgen and Klaus and were not popular with the group we met up with in Africa. Two of the men called Ndulu and Ali were our protectors and the whole group were very kind to us, but Ndulu and Ali were both killed by Jürgen and Klaus. They then came after us and, terrified, we ran into the jungle where, luckily for us, we bumped straight into a mercenary group of soldiers who shot Jürgen in the neck and then attacked the camp where we had been kept prisoner.

The point I'm making, Laura, is I was a dreadful wimp at that time but grew up rapidly when we were taken into the camp and saw the carnage with dead bodies strewn all around and most of whom had been very kind to us. It was horrible with flies buzzing in and around the bodies, almost making them appear to be moving. The air smelled of blood and it was a sweet, sickly smell which to this day turns my stomach when I think about it. We then went on with the mercenaries as they fought a group called the MPLA who were being supported by the Soviets. We stayed with the group known as UNITA until it seemed fruitless to continue, so two of the group decided that they needed to get us back home. On the flight back, the plane was hijacked but the mercenary who was called Daniel Knight managed to kill all three of the hijackers and had to fly the plane home because the pilot and co-pilot had been killed. As it turned out, George and I knew him because we had met before in a situation where he and his wife caught us throwing eggs at their kitchen window.

I am a different man now but I will say, the main reason I felt safe was because of the pursuit by the police and knowing there would be SWAT teams deployed who would not hesitate to shoot if they felt we were in danger of being killed. I know how professional the SWAT teams are and knew they would take them out. Had we been taken and nobody knew, I would have been much more concerned, not so much for me, but for Katie, plus if the worst did happen, the thought of Georgie being left alone in the world would have been unbearable.'

Laura asked whether or not they had ever seen a film called *The Out-of-Towners*, saying that Stuart's life seems to have followed a similar pattern.

Stuart began laughing at the memory.

'Is that where a man and his wife go for a job where everything goes wrong for them? They get mugged and are beset with one disaster after another and when they are safely on the plane going home, it gets hijacked?'

Laura agreed that it was and said that she could understand how he saw the funny side of it.

As the days progressed, so Katie's state of mind improved, notwithstanding that living with Stuart was always a laugh a minute. Although he would take life seriously when things needed to be dealt with properly, once he had dealt with the matter in hand, he would revert to being a natural comedian.

Within two weeks, she felt well enough to face the world again and so a return to see David Letterman to make an appearance was scheduled for three weeks later. This gave them time to put together their version of events from their ordeal.

On the night, the audience waited with enormous anticipation of seeing them again and when Letterman began to introduce them, they rose to their feet stamping, cheering and whistling even before they showed. When they did appear, the noise was deafening and continued, and even as Letterman made several attempts to quieten things down, he was failing miserably.

Stuart produced a black bag, and putting it over his head, he pretended to do karate moves on an unseen enemy and this made the audience laugh. Katie then put two fingers together as if to show she had a gun and put it against Stuart's head who began to move it left and right and up and down jerkily. She then quickly removed the black bag and he continued to look around and when he saw Katie's face, he made a loud, feminine scream and they both went to sit down.

They were asked several questions about their ordeal and they both managed to put a humorous slight on the events as they unfolded. Stuart managed to get a gag in regarding the disappearing head, saying, 'Now you see it, now you don't,' while the audience sat in an awed silence as they listened to them.

When asked whether this attack had anything to do with their sudden exit from the last show with Letterman, they explained that someone was out to get Katie's brother and they suspected that they wanted to get at him through Katie and his nephew Georgie.

'George and I go back a long way from just after we were born, and we have been almost like brothers since. We have both endured being kidnapped and taken to Africa where we were put amongst a group of rebels who were lovely people but two of them wanted us dead. One day, they saw an opportunity and we ran for our lives into the jungle and bumped into some mercenaries and the people we shared our evening meals with were slaughtered. So, as you can see, we have shared such a great deal together.

'I have been lucky to have been spotted and recruited as a comedian and also having Katie as my sidekick while George joined the Armed Forces with another close friend of ours called Ben. A couple of years ago, the person funding the African rebels was a man called Afolabi Okorie and I believe he had planned an attack on London which George, Ben and their colleagues had foiled, and I suspect that this might in some way be connected, I'm not sure.'

Naturally the audience wanted to know more but that was all Stuart effectively knew. He also felt that what had happened in Africa was well documented and so decided to change the subject, falling back into a much lighter mood and began fooling around again in the way that the Americans had grown to love.

They finished their interview with gags and a light-hearted look on their ordeal, finally letting the audience know that no matter what happens, America would remain their second home and the people their friends. They left to a standing ovation and cheers as they left promising to be back again very soon.

Meanwhile, back in the UK, on a lovely sunny morning with holidaymakers meandering around Southend-on-Sea, the peace was suddenly disturbed by what at first appeared to be a heavy thump that reverberated through the ground.

Chapter 8

Moments after the thump in the ground, a huge explosion was heard from the vicinity of Foulness Island where huge plumes of black smoke were seen to be rising.

The wind was catching it and blowing it out to the Thames Estuary. There was an eerie silence for a moment then, within minutes, the sound of sirens was heard some distance away which gradually got louder. The sirens seemed to continue for a long period of time, not leaving much to the imagination that this was serious. In Great Wakering, the police had cleared the roads, allowing all manner of emergency vehicles to pass through ranging from fire engines, ambulances, Bomb Disposal and then of course the police.

Inevitably, the local press were on the scene once the roads were cleared for local traffic who began to try to establish what had happened when a spokesman appeared and started to talk to them:

> 'Ladies and gentlemen, I am here to keep you informed as best I can but all I know at this moment is that an as yet untried explosive has detonated and there are two fatalities. Their families are being contacted and that is all I can tell you at the moment. There will be another briefing as soon as more information becomes available. Thank you.'

There was a flurry of questions, but the spokesman hurried back into the reception, leaving the press to their own assumptions.

An hour prior to the explosion, a black car with darkened windows had left Foulness Island and headed north to an Army barracks where Jayne and Ingrid had been given temporary accommodation and it was a complete surprise for them to see George and Murky alight from the car.

'Oh, my goodness, we were so worried because somehow, we had the feeling that the explosion had something to do with you!'

'Hugs and kisses first and explanations later!'

They embraced and finally went inside where teas and coffees were made.

It was Murky who began to explain that the explosion had been rigged and that now they were both hidden away, there was to be another bulletin at three in the afternoon. They turned the television on and five minutes later, the bulletin began.

> 'Good afternoon, my name is Andrew Jackson, and this is the news at midday.
>
> The pound has risen sharply to a five-year high and trade talks with China have ended with a twenty-billion-pound order for a fleet of Jaguar cars and other trading agreements, but first we are headed to Southend-on-Sea where our correspondent Nicholas Harris has an update on that explosion on Foulness Island.
>
> Nicholas, I believe you have an update on the situation on Foulness?'
>
> 'Yes, I do and good afternoon, everyone. I attended a briefing about twenty minutes ago and I can now confirm the names of the fatalities as their families have now been informed of this tragedy. They are George O'Rourke and David Murphy, also known as Murky, who were experimenting with a new type of explosive that was known to be highly volatile. The actual material has not

been announced as it is a secret concoction of several explosive elements. That's all I have at the moment so it's back to you at the studio, Andrew.'

All four sat quietly for a moment and it was George who broke the silence.

'It seems the news of our death is a bit premature.'

Ingrid was clinging to Murky and Jayne was clearly upset.

'Crikey, girls, it isn't true, you know, and we are not ghosts. Why are you so upset?'

Jayne called George an insensitive bastard and began pummelling him with a cushion.

'What part about that news bulletin do you think is OK? Ingrid and I have been waiting here not knowing how you are, where you are or whether or not there is a news blackout because you might be in serious danger. It's hardly like that either of you are in a cosy nine-to-five job! We have been sitting here night after night expecting news like that and hoping beyond hope that it never comes. You have no idea the dark places we've been to in our minds, not to mention sleepless nights, so don't you dare make light of it!'

George managed to grab the cushion, but Jayne was letting out all her frustration and began to pummel him on the chest. She wasn't hurting him and so he let her carry on knowing she would stop soon enough which she did by flinging her arms around him. She started to sob as her hysteria began to subside and he put his arms around her, hugging her tight.

'I am so sorry, poppet, I was very insensitive and wasn't thinking, we'll explain all once we're settled in. Shall we have a cup of tea and some biscuits?'

Ingrid looked up at Murky who appeared to be smiling at George's plight, and she elbowed him in the ribs saying if he was about to say something smart to think about it again.

'If I vent my feelings on you, I won't be able to stop, so keep whatever you were going to say to yourself.'

Murky sensed that the tension had run its course and said that he was only going to say how nice it was to be back with their wives and after such a lovely welcome. This earned him another dig in the ribs, causing George to snigger.

Jayne looked at George and began to chuckle, causing them all to start laughing. It wasn't hysterical but clearly a little over the top, releasing all the built-up tension and anxiety.

Once they had all settled down to a cup of tea, George and Murky started to explain why their accident had been fabricated.

'The thing is, guys, as you know George's friend, sister and nephew had been abducted by a group in the States, so in order to keep them safe, the accident was made to look like it was fatal.'

'Have Katie and Stuart been informed that it's all subterfuge and that you are both in fact safe?'

This time it was George who answered.

'Now this is the thing, it has to look authentic for obvious reasons!'

'So, the answer is no; that is so insensitive, poor Katie and Stuart!'

'I know it's horrible but think about it and why it is necessary. If we inform the American authorities who in turn tell Katie etc., it could inadvertently be leaked since it wouldn't be just the one individual who would have that information. Both Stuart and Katie are extremely popular in the States and the public are always hungry to hear as much news about them as possible. I am not being disparaging about US security, but it would take only one word out of place to blow the whole thing out of the water. Added to this is the fact that, as bad as it is, they have to look wretched as they leave the US to attend the inevitable religious ceremony, and as clever and good as they are at comedy, they would never be able to pull off pretending to be devastated.'

Both George and Murky were at pains not to mention the words 'funeral' or 'wake' in order not to upset their wives, but also in some way not wanting to tempt fate.

'They won't have heard about the accident yet and won't know for another couple of hours or so unless they are watching early morning television. They're in British Columbia at the moment performing in Victoria on Vancouver Island.'

'Now, once they are back in the UK, they are bound to want to contact both you girls, but because of the need for your personal safety and that of your families, they will be unable to make contact with you. I know it has been hard keeping you cooped up here for so long without speaking to anyone else apart from each other, but the alternative is unthinkable. This is an international gang with what would appear to be active contacts everywhere, and I can't run the risk of thinking about you in the hands of these evil bastards. Having seen what they did to Ben stills makes me sick to the stomach. Now, you won't get to see them until all the ceremonies are conducted and so it is an absolute must that you appear to be totally and utterly devastated.'

'Are they going to be told the truth once they're here and are your close families having their minds put at ease?'

It was Murky who answered.

'Sadly, no! It is imperative that the appearance of their losing us be kept up. Now the enemy hopefully think that George and I are out of the way and so we are going to take the fight to them with maximum backup so the risk to us is minimal.'

Both men looked at their wives and could see they were getting upset and understood why and so suggested that they have a meal and talk about it later.

'Guys, I can't cope with what's on my mind as it is, and I'm sure Inky would agree with me, that unless you can give us something that will put our minds at rest, we are going to have nightmares.'

'OK! We can only tell you the skeleton of what's planned but please be assured we won't be in too much danger ourselves. (George knew that this wasn't strictly true, but he had to somehow put their minds at rest.) The reason is that we are now certain of what they plan to do, and we have a very good idea of how to deal with it. Now there are six of us working together, three of whom are divers and they are the ones facing the most danger.

Finally, they settled down and chatted at just about anything and everything until the inevitable question was asked about how long the men were likely to be at their quarters; it was a question neither could answer.

'All we know is that we will not be leaving the barracks until we've been briefed. Major Bradley will be coming to see us with the rest of the team in the next few days so I expect we will all meet in the conference room and find out what's to be done and that's all we know. So let's settle down and enjoy the moment and what ingredients have you guys got? Anything that could be made into a shit-hot curry accompanied by copious amounts of booze?'

Since both Inky and Jayne enjoyed a spicy meal, there was no problem with food, but all they had was wine.

Murky did the cooking while George got the rice underway and by the time it came to serve up, they were all slightly pickled which had lightened the mood considerably.

Chapter 9

It was eight-thirty in the morning in Vancouver, and Stewart and Katy were enjoying their breakfast. They had had a wonderful evening performing at the Royal Theatre on Vancouver Island.

They had enjoyed a rapturous welcome and a standing ovation as they left the stage, and while it was no stranger to them to be treated in this way, it always left them with a warm feeling which they never took for granted. There was no end to their repertoire, and it was their ability to ad-lib throughout the whole show that endeared them to any audience no matter where they were performing.

They were discussing how they were going to address their next show which was scheduled in three days' time when the phone rang.

They always playfully argued about who should answer it, but on this occasion it was Stuart who picked up.

'Hello, Stewart Baxter speaking!'

There was a long silence as Stuart was trying to digest the news he was being given. He put the phone down and just stood there completely numbed.

By this time Katy was aware that something was wrong and began to question Stuart quite forcefully. The silence was setting her mind into overdrive and she asked again.

'Stuart, please for goodness' sake say something.'

He turned around and took Katy's hand suggesting that she sit down.

'Oh, my darling girl, I don't know how to tell you this but George and Murky have been killed in an accident. Apparently, they were both experimenting with a new explosive and it somehow blew up, killing them both. Apparently, someone will be coming to speak to us this evening.'

Katy just sat there saying nothing, but Stuart could see great orbs of tears developing in the corner of her eye and then she buried her head in her hands and began to sob.

'I don't understand it, he was supposed to be retired from active duty and he was only doing Major Bradley a favour by being seconded to the American DEA. He somehow had some skills that the Americans wanted to learn and then he was supposed to go back to teaching; God knows he deserved to lead a peaceful life after his distinguished service to his country.'

She was openly crying now, and Stuart was unable to console her while at the same time holding back his own tears. He and George had been friends since they were very young with another boy called Ben. Ben was horribly and sadistically mutilated by a wealthy West African called Afolabi Okorie. Okorie had played a significant part in the lives of Stuart and George since they were teenagers, and now Stuart was trying to cope with the loss of the last of his boyhood friends.

Katy could feel Stuart's body heaving and she gave him a big hug, saying that she knew George was like a big brother to him and how sorry she was.

'It just isn't fair; he's faced all kinds of danger and even survived an attempt on his life and now it all ends in a silly experiment with explosives!'

'We'll find out more when whoever comes to see us and explain what's happened.'

'What's the point? It won't bring either of them back, Oh Stuart, this is horrible.'

Little Georgie toddled up to his mum and dad asking why they were both crying.

They did their best to comfort him and asked Nanny if she could take him out for a little while.

Later that evening, it was Major Bradley who called with a lady who introduced herself as Cheryl.

'I can't begin to tell you how sorry I am for your dreadful loss; it hasn't been fully investigated yet as to what happened but apart from your dreadful sadness, they will be a terrible loss to their country. Please may I introduce you to Cheryl who is a grief counsellor and she has come to try and offer any comfort she is able to give.'

This was too much for Katy because she blamed her brother's death on Charles Bradley and really laid into him verbally.

'How dare you come here and try to offer us comfort when you are to blame for his death. He had already served his country with distinction when he retired and became a teacher but then the attempt on his life brought him back into active service. This was just to prevent an attack on the UK which he and his colleagues successfully foiled where dear Ben was horribly murdered. Then you persuaded George to help you again and now he is dead. If you don't mind, I would rather you left us in peace.'

Cheryl was about to say something but to avoid another outburst from Katy, Stuart said he was grateful for their coming all this way but suggested it might be best at the moment for them to leave.

Once again, Charles Bradley and Cheryl offered their condolences and quietly left, leaving a contact number in order that, should they wish to talk about it, they would be available to discuss it at another time.

Once everyone had left, Stuart and Katy both sat down together, not wanting to talk, and all that could be heard was the ticking of the clock, which seemed to be very loud, and Katy quietly sobbing.

After about half an hour, she was just feeling numb and, for the time being, all cried out.

'I can't believe it, Stoopot today started out so well with us joking around and within two minutes, everything just changed. I can't believe it has happened, I mean from what I understand, George and Murky have always been extra precautious when dealing with dangerous substances; it just isn't like them to be careless.'

Stuart for his part was desperately trying hard to hold it together while at the same time trying to comfort his wife.

'The thing is, my darling, we will have to accept life without George from now on and remember that we're not the only ones grieving for this terrible situation. Both our parents and Murky's folks will be devastated along with their wives and all those associated with the two of them.'

The mention of life without George set Katy to start crying again with Stuart aching at the loss of his lifelong and dearest friend. While he had come to terms with losing Ben, this was a terrible blow and despite being in an ecstatically wonderful relationship with a beautiful wife and little boy, he suddenly felt quite lonely. Eventually he felt the need to be more practical regarding their future and said that he would contact their agent in the morning.

'The thing is, sweetheart, we have made enough money to see us through three lifetimes and if you want us to go back home for good, that would be fine by me.'

Katy thought about it for a minute and asked how Stuart would really feel about that.

'I would really miss America and the American people. It's not where I want to retire but I really haven't got it out of my system. I have to say that although George was my best friend, he was your brother, too, so really, it's up to you.'

'I think it's a bit early to be planning that far ahead, Stoopot, let's try and get our heads around what's happened, so phone Ed Jackson to let him know we need to postpone our tour for the foreseeable future.'

'I really don't feel like talking to our agent today, I'll do it in the morning.'

They then poured themselves a drink and sat reminiscing about the wonderful times they all shared together when they were younger.

A little later, Nanny and little Georgie had returned and, seeing his little face together with having had a drink, they felt a bit more relaxed but still felt wretched inside.

Chapter 10

On arriving back in the UK, Charles Bradley went straight round to see Murky, Ingrid, Jayne and George to explain what had happened.

'I'm afraid that I was asked to leave: in fact, Katy really laid into me, blaming me for what has happened. Cheryl Cooper had accompanied me, and her speciality is grief counselling, and she managed to talk them around about letting her help them. She hasn't contacted me yet as to how well things are going but how do you try to get someone to accept the tragic loss of people you love?'

'Only they haven't lost them, have they? The poor buggers are grieving their hearts out thinking that George and Murky are both dead? This is so cruel; is there no way we can let them know?'

'My dear Jayne, it took a lot of arm-bending to persuade me to let you both know the truth so please don't make me regret it. If we let anyone else in on the secret, there is a greater chance for you both to be reliving what's happening now: only next time it could be for real.'

All four of them accepted this logic, albeit reluctantly, with both the men understanding why it had to be this way.

'Now we have to get down to the next stage and that is your supposed funerals. Your mother and father have been informed, George, and as I understand it, they want to arrange it with Murky's parents.'

'How are our parents? This gets worse by the minute. I mean, don't get me wrong but they are not youngsters and this news will totally destroy them. I mean, how long will this subterfuge need to last, sir?'

'No need to call me 'Sir' George now that, once this is all over and done, we will not be calling on either of you again under any circumstance. You have been asked to help because of your past dealings with the Okories. You know your way around the *Ardent Ventura* because the specs for the *Ventura* and *Voyager* are identical. Both inside and out. We have this from the yard that built them. As for how long will this last, we have a plan of action which will be briefed to you both in a few days. First, we have to get over this business of the funeral. Now then, ladies, you are both going to have to look totally devastated, and Ingrid, I would like you to try and get as close to the press as you can without appearing to do it deliberately and weep and say something like you have only just married and now, he's been taken from me. I can't emphasise enough the need for you both to appear totally heartbroken and devastated.'

'That won't be difficult, Major, just seeing all our families being totally crushed and distraught will be enough to set me off and I'm sure Jayne will feel the same way.'

Jayne was quietly weeping in her chair at the thought of the funeral and how the family was going to react.

'At the actual service I know I will be visibly upset but I'm worried that at the wake, where people mingle and have become much more settled and relaxed due to alcohol etc., I might not be able to keep up the pretence.'

'If that should happen to either of you and you begin to feel euphoric that you know your husbands are actually alive and well, seek each other out and come to me. I will get you out and tell everybody that you couldn't cope, and I will give everyone your apologies. Now, I don't think there is any more we can achieve here at the moment so with respect I will take my leave. You have four days, gentlemen, and I will send for you to attend a briefing in order that we can go over the plan that we have decided on.'

Not having been with their wives for some time, they welcomed the four-day respite where they could relax together, albeit in a military camp where entertainment was limited; but there was a cinema and a well-stocked mini-market.

During daytime hours, the boys remained inside their quarters just in case a quadcopter was flown over the site and even then, late in the evening, they would make every attempt to hide their identities, although the chances of being recognised were negligible since the campus was huge and full of different personnel from different areas of the Armed Forces.

There were many females as well, so Jayne and Ingrid didn't look out of place.

Since all four of them were accomplished cooks and with a good supply of alcohol, they just enjoyed entertaining themselves, together with the odd night out to see a film.

Although they were reasonably content, the girls especially were getting cabin fever and, as the days wore on, getting closer for the men to leave for their briefing, they were becoming quite melancholy. They both knew that when the boys left, they could be sent into action, and they could soon be reliving the recent scenario for real. The thought of being cooped up for an unspecified period of time only fuelled their innermost thoughts. Added to which there was the fear of what might happen and also their need for pretence at the funeral.

These and a thousand thoughts were constantly passing through their minds. They didn't share these thoughts with George or Murky, knowing they had a big enough burden of their own to shoulder.

It was in fact five days later when Charles Bradley returned, which did annoy the four of them since they had been expecting the major the previous day. They had spent the whole time anxiously waiting for the call while it could have been a bit more relaxing.

'My apologies, everyone, I can just imagine you must all have been on tenterhooks waiting for contact. The truth is that we did despatch a car yesterday but the wretched thing broke down, added to which, of the four other members due to arrive yesterday, two were delayed because of some fool jumping off the bridge straight in front of their train. If these people realised the awful mess they make around the surrounding area with blood, snot and tears, I'm sure they would think again. Anyway, I'm here now, gentlemen, so I will wait in the car outside and give you all a few minutes to gather your things etc.'

The atmosphere in the quarters was one of apprehension, with the girls both clearly upset, wanting them both to leave quickly while at the same time wishing they weren't going at all.

They hugged each other, with the girls making their husbands promise not to take any unnecessary risks with a final tearful farewell.

Murky said to George that if he got through this unscathed, he would be definitely retiring from active duty for good.

George agreed and said that he felt they were pushing their luck, considering all the scrapes they had both been through over the last few years.

Chapter 11

The major took them straight to the conference room where Jeremy, Steve, Brendan and Chizoba were already seated and, much to Murky and George's surprise, Jonah was also present.

Emma Belchin was also there standing at the front waiting while they all greeted each other and then called the meeting to order.

'I know you are all wondering why Jonah is here but I have included him because he is the best interrogator in the business. The reason that we are now ready to move on Okorie is because Jonah here together with Brendan managed to grab one of Okorie's henchman whom they followed when he left the *Ventura*. He took a cab and went to Southend-on-Sea where he got out just about opposite the *Richard Montgomery* and began observing it through very strong binoculars and taking notes. Brendan walked over to him, pretending to be a holidaymaker, and asked what he was looking at. The person spoke in a South African accent and explained he was conducting a survey on the sunken ship because he believed it contained gold bars and he was going to seek permission to make a dive on the ship and recover the gold for a small commission.

'At this point, Jonah innocently walked up to the two of them, and whilst concealing a Fairbairn Sykes dagger, he poked it into the soft flesh between the ribs and hip bone enough to hurt but not enough to penetrate the skin. He was told to walk towards their car which he had the good sense to do. They drove into Foulness Island where Jonah interrogated him; he was reluctant to begin with but Jonah persuaded him to talk.' George couldn't resist shouting out how many fingers did he have left which raised a laugh since nearly all present knew of Jonah's methods. Emma Belchin waited a while to let everyone settle down and began to say what they had discovered.

'Before I begin to explain, we were left with a bit of a dilemma because if the gentleman in question, who we discovered was called Pik Pferstanshaw, didn't return to the *Ventura* within a reasonable time, it would raise suspicions that he had been taken, which stood the chance of blowing the whole thing out of the water, so to speak.

We had to employ very unethical methods to throw Okorie and Co off the scent by staging a road traffic accident where the gentleman in question had been standing. We went to the local morgue and after pulling quite a few strings managed to obtain a recently deceased gentleman whom we drove to the spot where he was making his observations and arranged to have another car run into the host car. It was done in such a way that the way the cars were positioned, it wasn't difficult to remove the body from the car without being seen. The Air Ambulance was scrambled and collected the body flying to the hospital.

When Pferstanshaw was offered his clothes back from the body, he naturally declined so he is now dressed in Army fatigues.

The body was taken to an isolated ward and rigged up with all manner of apparatus that completely hid all his features so that when the inevitable visitor arrived, he would be unrecognisable.

The police are soon to put out a bulletin speaking about the accident and appealing for witnesses. It has been agreed they will report that a man in his thirties has been arrested on suspicion of dangerous driving. It is hoped that this will remove any doubts on Okorie's mind, especially when all Pferstanshaw's belongings will be offered to whomever turns up at the hospital. This, together with his torn clothing commensurate with an RTA, and attempts to save his life at the roadside should be very convincing. Any questions?'

There was a murmur in the room and Chizoba raised his hand, saying he didn't really understand the relevance about the fate of the South African and really wanted to know the plan of attack.

'In reality, Chizoba, there is no relevance, but I thought you might all like to know about the source of our information and why we are suggesting the kind of action we should take. Once Jonah here had finished his interrogation, Pferstanshaw sang like a soprano and not for the reasons you might think. Torture wasn't even necessary as Jonah can be very intimidating and as you may now have guessed, the target is definitely *the Richard Montgomery*. It is estimated that should the aging ammunition detonate, it is widely believed that it could create a tidal surge that could reach the very heart of London. We also know the date when the attack is likely to take place which is a week from the day after tomorrow, which is quite a high tide with the aim to cause maximum damage. This all does rather depend on whether or not the body that we commandeered is enough to convince the inevitable visit by Okorie's cronies that it was just an accident and not their security having been breached. To that end, gentlemen, you will all be staying aboard the *Broadbeam* which is a fairly luxurious 50-footer with all the mod cons on-board and even has a chef.' There was a general nod of approval when it was shown on the screen, since it did look magnificent although it would be dwarfed by the *Ventura*. 'You will be pootling around the area and quite a distance from the *Ventura,* but it has an extremely powerful engine that can deliver you all to your action stations very quickly. In the event that we have a 'go' situation which will be triggered by any unusual activity on-board their vessel, Team Maritime will don their SCUBA gear and an electronically propelled machine will be given to each one of you that will allow you to patrol specific segments around the exclusion zone.'

An aerial photograph was then displayed showing where each of the three divers would be patrolling their specific areas of operation.

'You will naturally all be armed with knives and harpoon guns should you find yourselves unable to get close enough for the kill.

This is a 'no prisoner' operation, gentlemen, since we don't have time for niceties. Team Land, you will, at the same time, board a RIB and be taken close to the *Ventura* and you will be armed to the teeth. You will, however, not open fire until there is absolutely no doubt that an attack is imminent. You will all have your favoured personal weapons together with small arms and shoulder-launched missiles. You will be required to board the ship and neutralise all the crew, including Okorie, killing anyone who makes any threats against your team. Now are there any questions?'

Murky wanted to know whether or not they had enough to arrest the whole group and impound the ship given that they had a witness.

'Unfortunately, Murky, he will no doubt claim he was coerced and threatened. Knowing something isn't the same as having tangible proof, and so I'm afraid this is the only avenue, risky as it is. If anyone can add to it to improve our chances of success, please speak now.'

There was silence until Jonah raised his hand, asking if he could be a part of it, but Charles Bradley declined his request.

'I'm really sorry, Jonah, because you have proven time and again how good an all-round operative you are but trying to board a ship from a RIB is bad enough without having had your kneecap blown half to bits. Well, if there is nothing else, we have a funeral to organise for George and Murky which is being scheduled to occur two hours after the wake. The reason for this decision is that it will no doubt be observed by one of Okorie's cronies which could provide us with an element of subterfuge. Once I have spent a reasonable time at your simulated funerals and wakes, I will quickly return to this office to control operations with Ms Belchin and the team. Thank you all, and from tomorrow morning you will be aboard the *Broadbeam*. Good day to you all and since I doubt I will see you again until the debrief, I wish you all Godspeed and the very best of luck.'

Chapter 12

Ingrid and Jayne were requested to make all the arrangements for their husband's phony funerals, and since it was considered safe for them to leave the security of the military base, Jayne invited Ingrid to stay with her while they made all the necessary preparations.

It was decided to have the funeral in Southampton as it seemed the most central crematorium to all those wanting to attend. Although they both knew that it wasn't for real, the thought that their husbands would soon be facing a great deal of danger weighed heavily on their minds.

Once all preparations had been completed, it was arranged that Murky's hearse would leave from his parents' house in Andover where Ingrid's family, who had just flown in from Poland, were staying; and George's hearse would leave from his house. It was going to be coordinated so that both funeral processions would arrive at the crematorium at the same time and they were both to be cremated with full military honours.

Ingrid was finding it difficult to appear that upset and devastated because her family didn't get to see Murky very often, and their feelings of grief were mainly centred on Ingrid and her tragic loss. Having said that, both Ingrid and Jayne did have heavy hearts, hoping to goodness that their husbands' mission would go as planned and that they wouldn't be doing this for real in a few days' time. Her entourage consisted of two cars and the hearse, with one car containing Murky's family, and a second with Ingrid and her family.

Jayne for her part wasn't finding it difficult to appear distraught because seeing his family looking absolutely devastated and totally miserable really upset her. She was so tempted to tell them the truth but knew she had to heed Major Bradley's warning about how dangerous it would be for the operation that was to coincide with the service.

As both processions turned into the grounds and on to the chapel, the number of the congregation was absolutely enormous. Naturally a great number of their comrades wanted to pay their respects together with the Guard of Honour, but it was the close friends and family that caused both the so-called widows to finally crack and be completely distraught and upset. For example, seeing Katy and Stuart literally totally broken and weeping uncontrollably was terrible. There were so many old faces from the past such as Bernhardt von Austerlitz who kept Stuart and George safe during their capture by an arms-smuggling gang headed up by Afolabi Okorie, Adwin's younger brother. Danny and Dawn Knight were there with Hendrik Van Hove who had eventually rescued the boys and even Allan who had talked George down while attempting to fly a plane back to England after he had foiled an attempt to hijack it.

As the coffins were removed from the hearse the sense of grief and sadness was almost tangible. The chapel was filled to capacity with people crammed in and around the walls.

The service told of all the adventures they had shared, with eulogies by family members. Major Bradley told the congregation about elements of their service to their country, and Danny Knight reflected how he had first met George and Stuart as young boys when they threw an egg at his kitchen window. Jonah and his wife were there and Jonah was the only surviving member of what was once a formidable team of four operatives.

All the families were naturally the first to vacate the chapel once the service had ended with the tune 'I give to thee my country' and walked past the dedications and flowers with a magnificent display by their regiment. Once they had got to the end of the display, they waited as all the guests filed past offering their condolences. As the guests finished talking to the families, they were requested to spread out in order to give the Guard of Honour enough space to carry out their last respects. The Guard of Honour conducted a very snappy drill in the grounds because at the request of the crematorium, no guns were to be fired.

The two *widows* and Katie were making attempts to smile, and while Katie was clearly distraught at the loss of her brother, Jayne and Ingrid were not finding it difficult to appear equally upset. Seeing all the family whom they loved looking completely and utterly devastated and lost made the atmosphere very sombre and sad.

Then it all became too much for Katie who suddenly broke down and began crying uncontrollably. Both Ingrid and Jayne moved closer to her to try to comfort her, but her distress went extremely deep as she tried to say all the things they all did together as youngsters. She was really breaking her heart since she adored her brother and his loss was too much to bear. She always knew that the line of work he was in was dangerous but never imagined that this would actually happen.

'I thought I had lost him when he got kidnapped by the arms-smuggling gang all those years ago, and now I have; forever.'

It began to get too much and began to affect the other two girls as well, and so they, too, began crying.

The thee of them looked a rare sight all dressed in black and, despite the tears, they were all stunningly beautiful and some of the male mourners made a point of getting a little closer to the three of them, much to the annoyance of their wives.

As the people began to leave, Charles Bradley noticed somebody standing in the grounds, not for any reason other than he had been there before the hearses had arrived and seemed to be paying a great deal of attention to the people who had begun to congregate at the chapel. He was carefully scrutinising every male as they were leaving, but Charles Bradley soon realised that he must have had a camera secreted somewhere in his clothes and he was photographing all of them.

He alerted his team and then approached the stranger. He was quite a tall man wearing a coat that looked a little too big and so assumed that it was a means of keeping the camera hidden.

'Did you know the deceased well?'

The major's approach took the man by surprise and so he jumped, and the major had expected that he might have tried to make a run for his car, but instead turned to greet him with an outstretched hand.

'Howdee, my name is Jacob Edwards and I'm here because I was in England and had heard about the two fatal accidents and wanted to come along. Since there was no room for me in the chapel, I decided to wait outside. To answer your question, no, I didn't know either of them.'

'Then I have to ask why an American who doesn't know either of them would be so interested. Now, I am assuming you are from the press: if that is so, you are behaving very suspiciously. There is one other thing that is really bothering me and that is: why you are taking photos of all the males attending? That IS a camera you are hiding under your coat, I assume? I'm afraid that since I don't know who the hell you are I'm going to have to confiscate the camera and you need some pretty good reasons to be here doing whatever it is you are doing.'

'My sincere apologies and I assume I am talking to Major Bradley. I am not with the press but the CIA. Can we talk somewhere quietly?'

Chapter 13

Since the coordinated attack on Okorie's ship was literally just hours away, Charles Bradley decided he didn't have time to take Edwards back to his office and so he rang the Guardroom of 457 Yeomanry Battery. It was quite close to the cemetery and requested that a room be made available in order to interview Edwards.

Prior to entering the room, Edwards was asked to produce his identification which was duly handed to the duty officer. He was asked to email a copy to his office and have it checked out.

Once ensconced in the room he asked Edwards to sit on a chair opposite and he had requested that some refreshments be sent to the room and that a guard be stationed outside the room.

'Did I hear you say refreshments and a guard? Surely that isn't necessary. I wouldn't have thought that this will take more than a few minutes because I have somewhere to be.' Instead, could I leave you a forwarding address where I could easily be contacted?'

'I have yet to establish firstly that you are who you say you are; secondly, if the CIA are involved, why have they not been in contact with my department, and finally what exactly is your interest in our business? So where to begin? In fact, why don't you tell me the reason why you are here, that would be a good start.'

'OK, fair cop; I am a CIA agent but not here on CIA business. It appears that your department and I have a mutual interest in a family called the Okories and have become aware that Adwin Okorie is headed for these shores.'

'That opens up more questions than it answers. That, for example, doesn't explain why you seemed so interested in the funeral of two of my operatives'!

'While I hadn't met either of them, I am aware that one was called George O'Rourke who, as a young boy, was captured by a gang headed by a West German agent, Bernhardt von Austerlitz. He had infiltrated the group to make sure that some very high-tech sniper sights didn't get to the intended recipients. The paymaster was Adwin's younger brother called Afolabi, and my interest at the time was how they got hold of the sights.'

'Have you ever met Bernhardt?'

'No! Why?'

'No reason, it's just that he was present at the service and if you had met him, he might have been interested in having a word with you.'

Charles Bradley was getting quite anxious because the meeting was now exceeding 30 minutes and he still hadn't got to the bottom of why Jacob Edwards was showing such an interest in the day's events.

With that, there was a tap on the door and a corporal entered with a document.

Charles Bradley excused himself as he opened it and began to read its contents.

> *Dear Major Bradley,*
> *Thank you for your enquiry regarding Jacob Edwards.*
> *He was indeed one of our agents but has since been suspended indefinitely. He is extremely resourceful, and I have to warn you that he is very dangerous. He has always borne a grudge against the man who he believes killed his father. Many years ago, his father Richard Edwards assumed the pseudonym of James Adams, and tried to infiltrate an arms-smuggling gang funded by a gentleman called Afolabi Okorie. He was an excellent*

CIA agent but within weeks, his cover was blown and, we believe, killed by a person from a West German agency called Bernhardt von Austerlitz. He had also infiltrated the gang and we believe von Austerlitz felt that Richard could have jeopardised the mission, hence his death.

His suspension is not related to his quest for revenge but mainly due to the way he interrogates suspects: it seems he enjoys it too much and some of the information he extracts turns out to be false. This is mainly because his victims confess to anything to stop him from continuing with their torment.

I am concerned that when he heard the news of the deaths of agents O'Rourke and Murphy, he wanted to find out who would be attending their funeral. If von Austerlitz plans to attend, I fear that he could possibly be in some considerable danger. To give you an example, when on active duty in North Korea he was captured and taken to a cell to be tortured but before any information could be extracted, he had killed three of his jailers and managed to escape the building and avoided being found. He turned up two days later in South Korea. He is extremely resourceful.

One other thing, he often travels with an accomplice, a beautiful woman known as Ubiytsa: the Assassin. She is of Russian descent and leads a perfectly normal life in Vancouver with her husband. He owns a successful trucking franchise in a place called Abbotsford. Since she semi-retired from active service, she is involved with volunteering for a local charity shop and to speak to her would not reveal her true capabilities. She is charming, witty and extremely knowledgeable. She was born Debbie Ann Cheveldeff, but since marrying Dean, she goes by the name of Debbie Barkman.

She left Canada a short time ago and caught a plane

*to Bulgaria where she has disappeared, if she is with
Edwards be exceptionally cautious: she is deadly.
Be very careful and keep a very close eye out for both
of them.*

I hope this helps.
Yours Aye,
Hamish Thorbin.

As Major Bradley took all this information in, he wasn't aware that
Edwards was watching him like a hawk and reading his reactions as
he read through the document.

Charles Bradley slowly folded the document, and as he placed it
in his jacket pocket, he looked up only to see the menace in Jacob
Edwards's face and realised he was about to attack. He tried to shout
a warning to the guard outside, but it was too late. Edwards was
over the top of the table, taking the major completely by surprise,
delivering a throat punch that although deflected by the major, still
disabled his ability to call out. Edwards then punched him in the face
and reached into his pocket, removing the document and also the
major's identity card. As he was struggling to regain his voice and
recover from the punch, Edwards left the room and told the guard
he had been released and he needed to leave on urgent business.

'I'm sorry, sir, but I have to have the major's authority first and
you need to be escorted...'

They were the last words he managed to say before Edwards
elbowed him in the temple, rendering him completely unconscious.

By this time, Charles Bradley had managed to compose himself
enough and left the room just in time to see Edwards about to exit
the building. Just before exiting, he activated the fire alarm and ran
out into the camp in an apparent state of panic.

He was challenged by a corporal but he appeared breathless and
told him that there were people inside the building who needed
urgent medical attention and raced towards the gate.

He hurriedly showed the guard Charles Bradley's ID card and

said that an incendiary device had been found in the building and he was going out to meet the emergency services. In the panic that Edwards displayed, the guard let him pass unhindered, but Major Bradley was almost at the gate. He shouted at the guard to stop Edwards, but it was too late, he had managed to secrete himself amongst the populace and got away.

Chapter 14

Charles Bradley was furious at himself for not being more careful: had he not been so lax and too engrossed in the message from America, he was more than capable of preventing Edwards from escaping.

The first thing he did was to contact Emma Belchin and requested that another team be activated. She quickly looked at her deployments and found a group who were doing surveillance duties. It was felt that to redeploy them temporarily would not jeopardise their own areas of operation.

Owing to the heightened mindset of the six agents about to go into action, it was decided that they should not be informed. The last thing Charles and Emma wanted was to have the concentration of the agents being distracted in order that they may focus on what could be an extremely dangerous mission.

The major made his way back to the wake, gave his apologies and left to deal with this new threat. Although not considered an immediate threat to the current operation, the last thing anyone wanted was to have one or possibly two loose cannons running around unchecked.

As soon as Charles Bradley entered his office, he made sure that he briefed the new team fully about the danger to Bernhardt von Austerlitz and that he *had* been contacted, warning him of the potential danger. He then told them he was going to go to the

German Embassy for his own safety and that the team stay in close proximity to wait and watch. There was to be a scrambled line where regular contact could be made at specific times of the day. Prior to leaving 457 Yeomanry Battery, the major had requested that the Americans send a photo of Edwards to his office which had already arrived, and each operative was given a copy.

'This is Edwards and be warned, he is highly dangerous and resourceful and there is a good chance he will be with a beautiful woman who is known as 'Ubiytsa' which I believe means 'the Assassin'. Don't let her beauty fool you, she is deadly.'

'If you have any questions, gentlemen, please be brief since there is a very pressing issue that I have to deal with urgently.'

'I have one, sir: do we know where von Austerlitz is at the moment?'

'He is still most likely at the wake and from there he will leave for the German Embassy which is where he will be taken. It is there that he will be at most risk. He is currently being protected by some of the attendees of the funeral until the Embassy manage to send a small squad of men to protect him along with you four while he is in transit. Although not still active as such, he still advises Ministers, and for all the work he has done and continues to do, he is held in very high regard by the German authorities. For him to be killed on British soil, although embarrassing for us, we would be devoid of a very useful and helpful friend.'

'He seems to require a heck of a lot of protection: exactly how dangerous is this Edwards?'

'Anyone who can be captured by the North Koreans, kill three of them with no weapons and escape from their dungeons has to be very dangerous. Now if that is all, I really must press on.'

There were no issues that the team required to know more about and so the major wished them all good luck and to keep the office informed of any developments.

Once ensconced in the Ops room, he was quickly briefed on progress.

'Hello, Charles, gosh you were cutting it a bit fine: what happened?'

'I'm afraid there has been another dimension added to the day but hopefully it shouldn't interfere with the current mission. I will update you after we have hopefully neutralised Okorie and his cronies.'

Emma Belchin acknowledged the major's explanation when suddenly *Broadbeam* broke radio silence.

It had been agreed that radio silence would be observed until ten minutes prior to the team on *Broadbeam* were due to begin their assault and there was still twenty minutes to go.

'Hello, Lima Charlie, this is *Broadbeam*, over.'

'Lima Charlie send, over.'

'Guests have begun arriving and reception party has gone out to meet them, over.'

'Lima Charlie understood, how many have been sent to welcome the guests and how close are you from the meeting point, over?'

'*Broadbeam* six sent and approximately four minutes away from time of despatch, over.'

'Lima Charlie, understood. Are there signs that the party is about to start?'

'*Broadbeam*, yes and it seems a swimming contest is about to get underway…wait; out!'

It was obvious that something had happened on *Ardent Ventura* that had prompted the team to deploy all six operatives.

'It would seem that we are now in a waiting game but there are two pressing issues we need to discuss. There is a rogue CIA agent on the loose who wants to kill Bernhardt von Austerlitz because he apparently murdered his father. Perversely it is all connected to our current situation but not in a direct way. It occurred many years ago in a debacle with Adwin's brother Afolabi. It is believed that he is travelling with a beautiful woman known as Ubiytsa who is an assassin. They've both gone to ground but we are keeping a very close eye on Bernhardt.

There is, I feel, a more important issue about how we deal with informing George and Murky's families that in fact their deaths had been staged for everyone's safety. It was abundantly clear that Adwin wanted to avenge himself not only on Great Britain, but also on Murky and George for killing his brother.

'Initially and not thinking it through properly, I thought that we could do it at a private function for close family only. Now the operation is underway, should anything happen to both of them it's best left as it is, but if one is killed and the other survives.'

'I hope you're not suggesting that in the event of that happening we eliminate the survivor. I mean, I know our line of work is dirty and almost at gutter level and it's for the sake of Britain's security. But I mean both those boys could not have served their country more loyally.'

'I'm not sure what you take me for, Emma: absolutely not. This isn't a rerun of *Capricorn One* but it is something we may need to consider on how we handle the situation in the event should it happen. The best outcome we could hope for is that there are no fatalities in any of our team.'

Chapter 15

The wake was winding down with guests leaving, and no one had noticed that Bernhardt had already left.

It was felt the occasion was solemn enough without adding any further complications.

He had been approached by the concierge of the hotel who explained that there were some gentlemen at reception who needed to speak to him. Bernhardt recognised two of them since they were part of the Embassy Protection Team and the other four were introduced as being members of MI6. At their request, the group were ushered into a side room where Bernhardt was briefed on the circumstances. Clearly the situation that had brought about the need for an early departure from the wake was very clear in Bernhardt's mind. He remembered that fateful night when he had killed a CIA agent. Although it was a necessity to keep the sniper sights safe and close to him, he did feel quite traumatised by it, and it was something that haunted him frequently. The problem was that he knew if he hadn't had acted when he did, the agent known as James Adams would more than likely have turned the tables on Bernhardt, not realising that he was West German intelligence. While the Americans have always been close allies of Great Britain, they would have very much liked to have the sights in their possession, plead innocence and claim them to be of their own design. The sights would more than likely have been dismantled to see what made them so special and copied. It wasn't personal, it was business. The Embassy Protection Team had requested that Bernhardt embark their car while MI6 would follow closely behind.

The journey to the German Embassy was relatively stress-free, although at one point the driver of the MI6 car thought they were being followed by a motorcyclist. It did seem to stay behind them for what seemed like an age, but eventually, once the road was clear, the bike overtook both cars and it was assumed they were sightseers as they went past. There was a girl on the pillion with her hair flowing out from under her helmet and one of the agents felt a touch of jealousy because he and his young wife loved motorbikes but had just had a child and a bike was no longer feasible.

They continued for a short while when the car in front suddenly swerved as it rounded a bend in the road.

The motorcyclists had crashed the bike and where under such circumstances when escorting someone they would continue and ring the Emergency Services, the accident looked as if it needed immediate assistance since the man was lying unconscious about ten feet from the bike, but the girl was nearer with blood all over her face and hands. An Embassy Protection Officer got out of the car and went to see to the unconscious biker, and an agent from MI6 went to see if he could help the girl. She was writhing around on the ground and suddenly from behind her back, she produced a pistol and thrust it just an inch from the man's face.

The driver of the car was about to react, and she shot at him with the bullet taking a chunk out of his ear. She was now standing and had them both covered with her pistol, telling them both not to do anything silly and they would live.

The Embassy car had been similarly compromised and all mobiles and means of communication rendered useless.

They were all told to park their cars properly and the bike was placed in front of the cars to give the appearance of a comfort break.

They were then told to sit on the verge and act normally.

'If anyone stops to ask if everything is alright, you will wave them on, understood?'

Allow us to introduce ourselves, My name is Jacob Edwards retired from the CIA and this is Debbie Ubiytsa and she is!'

Bernhardt interrupted, saying he knew who she was.

'Hello, Debbie, so we finally get to meet!'

'This is actually one Debbie Barkman who is a freelance assassin and operates mostly throughout Africa. She disposes of people deemed unsavoury to certain governments. I have been trying to make contact with you, Debbie, about a particular colleague of mine who worked with me years ago in Mozambique. He was called Joshua Reinfeldt and, although very young, he was a very reliable and trustworthy agent. He remained there after I left but I do know he was there at about the same time that you got rid of the rebel called Joshua Savratti.'

'Not that it matters but I have no idea who you are, but yes, I do know Joshua and he married a local girl and now owns a big farm.'

'Ah! You would more than likely know me as Heinrich Moeller!'

'So, you are the elusive Moeller.'

There was a sudden outburst of sheer anger as Edwards, who by now had had enough of the niceties, wanted to deal with Bernhardt.

'Once you two have finished your lovely little tête-à-tête, I have a massive grievance with you, von Austerlitz. You killed my father and left my mother so broken that she took her own life. Now you are going to fulfil my lifelong dream of revenge.'

'These people have no argument with you, so I suggest you let them go. We both know the authorities will know that whatever you intend doing will have been done by you so leaving witnesses won't make any difference!'

'I will once I've dealt with you, but before I do, I want to know why! Why did you kill my dad? You were both working on the same side, for God's sake… Why?'

'I'm afraid the answer to that is very convoluted and, having been an agent yourself, you will know what a dirty business we find ourselves in. I have nothing to lose so will just say that the British and West German Governments had developed some very high-tech sniper sights that were about to fall into the hands of an unsavoury arms-smuggler and it was sadly your father or me. I am so very sorry that I had to do it, so go ahead and do your worst.'

Edwards hesitated for a moment and it appeared as if he was having second thoughts, but then suddenly he turned with rage and hatred written all over his face and aimed his pistol at Bernhardt's head. But before he could pull the trigger, he suddenly collapsed on the floor, writhing in agony and holding his hip. This was followed a split second later by the report of a rifle as two armed men broke cover and came running towards the group.

They were from the Embassy and when Bernhardt hadn't shown when expected, they were despatched to see what had delayed them. They began shouting and ordering everyone to the ground and once everyone's identity had been verified, the two perpetrators were arrested. Bernhardt offered Debbie a handkerchief to wipe the blood off her face which she took and smiled saying it was pig's blood. The car that had been sent to find Bernhardt was then brought forward, and Debbie and Jacob Edwards were driven off with Edwards being taken to the hospital where he was to be guarded. They would both have to await whatever the authorities planned to do with him.

Chapter 16

'Hello, *Broadbeam*, this is Lima Charlie, send sitrep over!'

Broadbeam, three partygoers entered water at T minus three. The remaining three are about to invite themselves to the party and it appears that the party is getting well underway, over!'

'Lima Charlie understood…out!'

'Well, it seems that our teams have begun their assault and I'm sure you all join me in wishing them Godspeed!'

Emma Belchin ordered that the Thames Barrier be operated as a precaution and declared that it was now a waiting game.

The Defence Secretary, who was also in the room with his team of advisors, had naturally been briefed from the start. Initially, he wanted to know why the *Ventura* couldn't be just blown out of the water, but he accepted that it would likely set off an international incident where there was as yet no proof of Okorie's intentions.

'The thing is, Minister, although the Ghanaian Government knows he's a bad egg, he, like his brother before, managed to stay one step ahead of the authorities, and should we do something like that, the Ghanaian public would see it as an outrage against their country. Their government would then have to… Well, I don't think I need explain anymore because the outcome we know would be inevitable.'

There was a tap at the door and a note passed to Charles Bradley.

'Well, at least there is one bit of good news: Edwards and his assassin friend have been captured and Bernhardt von Austerlitz is safely ensconced in the German Embassy.'

Meanwhile at the scene of the *Richard Montgomery*, Jeremy, Steve and Chizoba had donned their diving gear and entered the water about a five-minute, power-aided swim from their target. At the same time George, Murky and Brendan cautiously approached the *Ventura* and began to observe the ship with binoculars. He saw five men throwing bundles over the side of the *Ventura,* and Brendan, being a superb marksman, started picking off the people on the deck. He had a high-powered rifle, and as the RIB opened up the throttle, he had either wounded or killed three of the deckhands before the others realised that they were under attack. This was followed by frenzied activity on-board where more people appeared on deck, and one appeared to have a grenade launcher. The launcher was fired but Murky quickly changed course and the missile flew harmlessly out to sea. They knew they had to get on-board as soon as possible to prevent the crew from passing any more bundles over the side which were assumed to be explosives. There was also the danger that, should more missiles be fired at them, while they could be avoided by manoeuvring the RIB, it could either cause serious damage or kill innocent people.

Before the crew on *Ventura* could load another grenade, the three agents in the RIB were now in range for their machine guns to bear. George and Brendan raked the deck and bridge, each emptying their magazines, reloading with fresh and continuing to pile as much metal into the *Ventura* as possible. Murky quickly manoeuvred the RIB alongside the stern of *Ventura* where the three of them scrambled aboard only to be met with small arms fire, and George felt he had been punched in the arm. A bullet had hit his left arm but luckily missed the bone, and being so pumped up with adrenalin, he stormed forward with Brendan and Murky, raking the whole area in front with a wall of lead. There were screams and groans as they went forward and noticed several wounded or dying men on the floor. Knowing they had to continue going forward, they knew they couldn't afford to have armed wounded men behind them, and so with the greatest reluctance, they killed them as they went past. One or two had run further into the ship but for now the lower deck was theirs.

They regrouped and cautiously got to the bottom of the stairs that Brendan and Murky climbed with George covering them both from behind. As they were about halfway up, a man brandishing an automatic pistol appeared at the top but George fired and the man's head disappeared in a crimson fountain, and as if in slow motion, started to collapse at the knees, falling down the stairs. The descent was quite rapid, making George sidestep the falling body.

Once they got to the top, there were only two people left standing. They had discarded their weapons and had their hands in the air, begging the agents not to shoot.

Murky forced them to their knees and looked menacingly at them, demanding to know how many armed men remained.

One of them suggested that they look around to see the carnage that had been caused. There were clearly at least twenty dead that could be seen but there was still uncertainty regarding elements of the gang still hidden.

'Where's Okorie?'

The one who spoke before pointed out of the window to a fast launch heading around the coast.

'He is in there and leaving us to face his consequences. He was to pay us well but only in the event that we succeeded in causing the ammo ship to detonate – bastard.'

Murky rushed to the bridge which was now deserted, and quickly reached for the ship's radio.

'Hello, Lima Charlie, this is Team Land, the *Ventura* is now captured, one team member slightly wounded with several dead perpetrators. Urgent request for backup to intercept fast launch heading east along the coast believed to contain Okorie...over!'

'Lima Charlie, Wilco wait out.'

Once the prisoners were bound, it was now a waiting game to see who would emerge from the sea.

'How many divers went over the side to plant the explosives?'

'There were supposed to be seven, but your attack caused panic and only two made it. Listen, I know I'm in real trouble, but I only did this for the money because my little sister got involved with selling drugs. She owed a lot of money to some really bad people and I have to help her out so I will testify against Okorie if it will go well with the authorities.'

Brendan said that he was afraid that the team couldn't help him but felt sure that he would get a fair hearing.

'Hello, Team Land, this is Lima Charlie, copter and launch despatched and came under heavy fire; the launch has been completely destroyed along with all on-board, there are no survivors, over.'

'Team Land...understood...out.'

Jeremy, Steve and Chizoba were having a great deal of difficulty in negotiating around the ammunition ship because of poor visibility, but Chizoba thought he detected movement just ahead and so cautiously moved forward. Suddenly, he was attacked where a pair of legs had straddled him, and his attacker attempted to cut through his breathing tube. Then a second attacker managed to pull the mouthpiece out of his mouth and hit his head with the hilt of his knife.

Slowly Chizoba began to sink into the abyss, and as the two attackers were about to surface, Steve fired his spear gun at one of them, hitting him in the groin, but the other one managed to break surface only to be met with the muzzle of a gun being brandished by Murky.

Jeremy began to dive frantically after Chizoba and all he had to go on was the line of bubbles emanating from below. He finally, by pure chance, saw Chizoba and managed to get to him, placing his mouthpiece into Chizoba's mouth and slowly started to get them both to the surface.

It was a miracle that he was still alive, although still groggy from the knock on his head and a lung half full of water.

Murky was interrogating the other diver, wanting to know whether or not he had primed the explosives and, if so, how much explosive was used.

At first he refused to answer but Murky had learned a few tricks from Jonah and without even touching him, he explained that only one of the bundles was caught but the detonators had been lost, and so apart from there being a few extra explosives in and around the *Richard Montgomery*, a potential disaster had been averted.

Chapter 17

Two days after the success of the mission and once all the debriefing was complete, Charles Bradley requested that a room in the hotel where the wake had taken place be made available. The families of George and Murky's were requested to attend what was described as a discussion.

There was a reluctance by Katie and Stuart, but both Ingrid and Jayne, who had been contacted immediately after the success of the mission, knew that apart from George's wound, they were unscathed.

Both girls managed to persuade the Baxters to attend.

Charles Bradley, feeling very awkward, addressed the gathering feeling that the best way to handle it was not to beat about the bush too much and so he began.

'For the first time in my life I find myself almost at a loss for words because what I am about to tell you is, to say the least, bizarre.

As you are all aware, there was an incident at Southend-on-Sea earlier this week which had everything to do with George and Murky and what they have been working on these last couple of months.

Now before I start, I'm sure you all know the kind of business that we find ourselves doing, but we must protect our country and its citizens at all costs. As a result, there is sometimes a need to employ a great deal of subterfuge; Oh dear, I am waffling on. OK, I'll not beat about the bush anymore: both George and Murky are in fact safe and well and waiting just outside the room and will come in once you have taken in what I have just said.'

Katie was in shock but did manage to compose herself to ask why they were put through this horrible experience.

'I am so very, very sorry, Katie, and of course all of you, but there were several reasons why it had to be done this way. Firstly, it became clear that a gentleman called Adwin Okorie wanted revenge on Great Britain because we foiled an attempt by his brother to attack London a few years ago. He also attempted to steal some extremely precious diamonds which was again foiled by us. I would rather not go into the reason why but Murky and George hunted Adwin's brother Afolabi down and killed him. Several attempts by Adwin have recently been made on Murky and George's lives in revenge for them killing his little brother. When those attempts failed, they changed their tactics and tried to get at them through friends and family, hence the failed attempt to kidnap Stuart and Katie. We had to fake their deaths to protect you, for which you have our sincere gratitude and apologies for putting you through such a terrible time.

'Now I know that there are two men outside the door who, when they enter, won't be mistaken as ghosts.'

The door opened and in walked both men who just stood there waiting for a reaction.

There was a long silence, with all the family members completely in shock. The two men whose funerals they had thought they attended two days before were not dead but just standing in front of them.

Numbly, Katie stood and began walking towards George. she then broke into a run and grabbed him, crying, and began hitting him then hugging him, not knowing what emotion to display next.

George had to restrain her because his arm, although a flesh wound, hurt like the devil.

George looked across at Murky and said, 'Why is it that every time a family member finds out I'm not dead, they start hitting me?'

Stuart who would normally come out with some witticism or

other found himself so elated that his childhood friend was alive and well and moved Katie aside to give his friend a big hug. The mood in the room had improved dramatically with Murky's family trying to get to him for their hugs. Both Jayne and Ingrid stood back to allow the others in the room to have their turn at greeting both men.

Charles Bradley then began to talk once the furore had quietened down.

'Ladies and gentlemen, you are all invited to a banquet in celebration that a big threat this country has been facing for some years is now eliminated. Now, before you all leave, it gives me great pleasure to announce that all six participants in this operation are to be honoured in the New Year's Honours List. Furthermore, George and Murky are hereby released from active service with a guarantee they will not be the first ones called for any future requirement.'

Epilogue

In the New Year's Honours Investiture, Charles Bradley became a Knight of the Realm and Emma Belchin made a Dame. Chizoba was awarded an Honorary British Empire Medal. Brendan, Steve and Jeremy, who had served with honour in many other conflicts, were all OBEs and George and Murky had a bar added to their GC ribbons.

George and Jayne were welcomed back into their respective schools, and knowing about George's experiences, the students were very attentive while in his class. For her part, Jayne also had quite a potted history, and her class, who were mainly from poorer families, enjoyed her lessons and adored her for being such a compassionate and understanding human being. She brought out the best in her students and their grades improved dramatically. She worked throughout both her pregnancies and returned to school shortly after the children were born.

Murky and Ingrid finally had a proper and well-attended wedding and moved to Poland. Murky got a job as a military advisor while Ingrid returned to her job as a scientist. They also had two children who were named George and Katie.

George, Murky, Stuart and Jonah with their families met regularly and remained the very best of friends for the rest of their lives.

Author's Note

Once again, a great deal of imagination has been used in this novel which contains a lot of inaccuracies. They are quite deliberate because this was never intended to be remotely construed as a true story, but as an escape from reality and for someone's reading pleasure.

When one writes a book, it is not necessarily done as a means for an income, and if it is read, it means that you have entered someone's world, albeit briefly. This venture started out some 30 years ago, when I wrote an autobiography followed by the intention to write a trilogy. Although there are three novels in this series (this being the last one), I don't feel it can be classed as a trilogy.

In the text, I referred to a statement that 'This isn't a rerun of *Capricorn One*'. It is a film made in 1977 about the USA faking a manned mission to Mars, but the astronauts are actually in a studio in America. The space module crashes on its way back to Earth and so, to prevent the ruse from being discovered, the authorities decide that the astronauts have to be killed.